Dear Reader

Welcome to the third book in my *New York Hospital Heartthrobs* trilogy. When I first learned I was going to write these books, I knew that I wanted a theme about the place to which we are all connected—home. I wanted to write stories about what compels people to want to go home, and what binds their hearts to that special place. In this group of stories it was the love of a generous woman who touched countless lives.

Cherished memories…that's what home is to me—and that's what home becomes for the heroes and heroines of *New York Hospital Heartthrobs*. When Rick Navarro came home it was to accept a job and, as a single dad, to make the best home possible for his son. That's Rick's entire world: his son, his job. Until single mum Summer Adair shows up. But then the past Rick wants to ignore rears up to haunt him in ways he never expected—and in the same way Summer's past won't let go of her. Yet in two single lives that seem to run parallel in so many ways, and still remain divided, there's a greater purpose—their children—to bring them together.

I've loved writing these three stories about what brings people home and how love enables them to stay there. And, as always, I love hearing from you, so please feel free to email me at Dianne@DianneDrake.com

Wishing you health and happiness!

Dianne

Now that her children have left home, **Dianne Drake** is finally finding the time to do some of the things she adores: gardening, cooking, reading, shopping for antiques. Her absolute passion in life, however, is adopting abandoned and abused animals. Right now Dianne and her husband, Joel, have a little menagerie of three dogs and two cats, but that's always subject to change. A former symphony orchestra member, Dianne now attends the symphony as a spectator several times a month and, when time permits, takes in an occasional football, basketball or hockey game.

THE
RUNAWAY NURSE

BY
DIANNE DRAKE

First published in Great Britain 2012
by Mills & Boon, an imprint of Harlequin (UK) Limited.
Large Print edition 2012
Harlequin (UK) Limited, Eton House,
18-24 Paradise Road, Richmond, Surrey TW9 1SR

© Dianne Despain 2012

ISBN: 978 0 263 22468 9

Harlequin (UK) policy is to use papers that are natural, renewable and recyclable products and made from wood grown in sustainable forests. The logging and manufacturing process conform to the legal environmental regulations of the country of origin.

Printed and bound in Great Britain
by CPI Antony Rowe, Chippenham, Wiltshire

Recent titles by the same author:

FIREFIGHTER WITH A FROZEN HEART**
THE DOCTOR'S REASON TO STAY**
FROM BROODING BOSS TO ADORING DAD
THE BABY WHO STOLE THE DOCTOR'S HEART*
CHRISTMAS MIRACLE: A FAMILY*
HIS MOTHERLESS LITTLE TWINS*
NEWBORN NEEDS A DAD*

***New York Hospital Heartthrobs*
**Mountain Village Hospital*

**These books are also available in ebook format
from www.millsandboon.co.uk**

CHAPTER ONE

"DADDY!"

Rick Navarro braced for the impact the instant he stepped through the door, and he wasn't disappointed when his son launched himself through the air straight into Rick's arms. This had been cute when Chris was two or three, even four. But he was six now, a big boy for his age at that, and Rick did have to admit that while he hated to break that tradition, Chris's little flying act now had the potential to knock the wind out of him if he didn't prepare himself for it. "Easy, sport," he said, as the boundless bundle of energy hit him dead center in the chest.

"Johnny Redmond let me ride Toffee today! All by myself! And I didn't fall off."

"You didn't? Well, that's great! " he said, sorry to have missed it. But duty called. He couldn't help it. Such was the life of a single dad and he hoped that someday, when he looked back, he wouldn't turn out to be one of those parents who could count the missed moments. Because he was trying to find the balance. Working hard at it. Some days succeeding, some days not. Tough jobs, being a dad, being the head of a hospital. Life was good, though. Not perfect, but good. "I hope somebody took some pictures," Rick said, easing his son to the ground.

"Lots of them. And a video. Mrs. Jenkins said you should be able to see the whole thing."

God bless Mrs. Jenkins for that. "I'm sorry I didn't get there," Rick said. "I really wanted to, but I couldn't leave the hospital. You did thank Mr. Redmond for letting you ride, though, didn't you?"

"Yes. And he said I could come back any time. And it's OK you didn't get there. You had to take care of sick people."

Age six, and Chris was so…wise. He wasn't sure what he'd done to deserve a kid this great, but there wasn't a day gone by he didn't thank God for his good fortune. Christopher Ricardo Navarro was the best thing that had ever happened to him, and he regretted nothing about the way he'd come to be a single dad. Not one single thing. "Did you go for ice cream afterwards?"

Chris shook his head. "Mrs. Jenkins said she was saving that for you since she's dia-dia…" He frowned, shrugged.

"Diabetic. Means she can't eat much sugar." Well, at least one bright spot in his day was opening up…a date at the ice-cream shop downtown. He glanced over Chris's shoulder to the portly older woman who was waving goodbye to him as she scooted out the back door. She was a treasure. Loved Chris, didn't mind the sometimes odd hours she was called on to take care of him. A literal godsend. But not a mother, and that's what made Rick feel guilty. Chris had never known a mother, never known the nurturing of another woman besides Mrs. Jenkins. To be sure, it was a loss, but not one Chris even recognized, as it had been just the two of them since the day of his birth. Father and son… "So, how about I go take a quick shower then we'll head on down to Benson's Ice Creamery and see what the flavor of the day is?"

"Chocolate chocolate," Chris said, resolutely. "That's what I want. Mrs. Jenkins let me call them and they told me it's chocolate chocolate. I want mine with chocolate sprinkles."

A boy who knew his own mind. Rick smiled with pride as he stepped around Chris and mussed the boy's curly black hair. "That's exactly what I want, too," he said. "With *extra* sprinkles." He was a lucky man. If only the lucky man could find a couple more hours every day to spend with his son, his life would be perfect. "Oh, and put on another shirt. That one looks like you've already had a little chocolate chocolate."

Summer Adair glanced in the front window of Benson's Ice Creamery, debating the expense. Actually, she was debating whether or not she could buy Alyssa a scoop of vanilla and not succumb to the temptation herself. Pennies counted these days. Especially lately, when there weren't so many of them coming in, and the ones she had saved were, of necessity, guarded carefully. Grace Corbett had left her a nice sum, enough to help her get by for a while if she was careful. Very generous, considering that Grace had been her employer, not a family member. And there was the cottage…that was a huge blessing. Small, and just on the edge of the Gracie Estate, it was perfect for her and Alyssa. More than that, it was all hers! Another instance of Grace's generosity. Her very own home…it was the first time she'd ever owned anything of her own outside a few trifles. With this new life and new opportunities simply handed to her, Summer was still a cautious woman in everything she did, including wasting money on a little treat for herself.

"Do you want some ice cream?" she asked Alyssa, positive her daughter, aged four, wouldn't say no, especially to the bright lights and pretty colors of Benson's—all designed to capture a child's eye. Sure, she bought ice cream at the grocery store occasionally. But, darn it, you had to indulge your child sometimes, didn't you? God knew, there hadn't been many indulgences for either her or Alyssa since Grace Corbett had died. But here she was, debating a scoop of ice cream like it was a new car she was purchasing. Thinking in those terms, it seemed a little silly, actually. Especially since it was for Alyssa.

"Ice cream, Mommy," Alyssa said, standing

on tiptoe to look into the parlor window. "Can we please go in?"

"Tough choices inside," a deep, familiar voice commented from over her shoulder.

Rather than turning to see him, she looked at Rick Navarro in the window's reflection, and bit the inside of her lip to keep herself from grinning a schoolgirl grin that stretched from ear to ear. She really liked Rick. Handsome man. Bronzed skin. Large, broad shoulders. To-die-for wavy black hair. Nice smile. A real breath-taker, if you were inclined to want your breath taken. Which she wasn't. Still, she was human. Flesh and blood, beating heart that was beating a couple ticks faster now that his breath was tickling the back of her neck. And he was a very nice view, even in reflection. Something she'd been trying not to notice for months. Failing miserably, however. "Not when you have a picky eater. She likes vanilla."

"No sprinkles?" he asked.

Summer shook her head. "So far she hasn't wandered into the world of sprinkles. I've tried keeping things a little more simple than that." She glanced at Chris, who was pointing out to

Alyssa a picture in Benson's window of an ice-cream cone with sprinkles. "Although I suppose it's coming, isn't it?"

"Probably sooner than you think. So, would you two ladies care to join us two gents for ice cream?" Rick asked. "With sprinkles?"

"Sprinkles?" Alyssa mimicked, pointing to the picture in the window. "Can I have sprinkles, too, Mommy?"

"You've started something," Summer said to Rick.

He tossed Summer a wink. "Wait until she knows she can have whipped cream and a cherry on top. That's when the fun really begins because it will lead to things like ice-cream sundaes, banana splits, milk shakes…"

"Oh, I think sprinkles are enough for one day." Did she look pathetic, gazing into the store longingly, nose pressed to the window? Or was Rick simply being kind? He was a nice man. Also, her boss, part time. So far, though, there hadn't been a reason for anything other than loosely casual, translated to mean safe at a distance—the way she tried to keep herself with everybody.

"Then it's an ice-cream date?"

OK, maybe not as loosely casual as she'd thought. But the word *date* startled her a little. She didn't date. *Wouldn't* date. Wouldn't budge on her position about that either. Of course, she was sure Rick hadn't meant anything by *date*. She was also sure she had to quit overreacting to things that weren't meant to be anything other than what they were. Like this. It was meant to be ice cream. Nothing more. Yet overreacting was a foible of her nature, more ingrained than she wanted it to be, especially these past couple of years. "An ice-cream…date. For one, though. I, um…I don't indulge."

"Only one?" Rick asked, holding the parlor door open for them. "Am I going to have to use some fancy persuasion to get you to change your mind?"

Chris went in first, and ran straight to the see-through display of all forty kinds of ice cream. Alyssa got caught up in the excitement and broke right away from her mother, which caused Summer to panic. She didn't let go of her daughter in public. Not ever. Too many things could go wrong in the blink of an eye, and while this was only a small ice-cream shop where nothing was more than a few feet away from her, the sensation of fear, mixed with the need to grab Alyssa and run, nearly doubled her over. She resisted the outward manifestations, of course. Over time, being a single mother, the way she was, she'd gotten good at putting on the right outward appearance for the occasion, even when her gut was knotting and her lungs were going into spasm. Like they were doing right now. "I'm not much of an ice-cream eater," she said stepping up behind Alyssa, who was busy peering into the case at all the different kinds of ice cream.

"What are these?" her daughter asked innocently, pointing to the virtual rainbow of colors.

Proof of a sheltered life, Summer thought, taking hold of Alyssa's hand, instantly feeling better. "Ice cream comes in different flavors, and different flavors come in different colors."

"Would you like some samples?" the boy on the other side of the case asked. He was about sixteen, seemed harmless. Wasn't paying more attention to one person than another, Summer noted, finally relaxing a little.

"She likes vanilla," Summer said, deliberately not looking at the disappointment she knew would be registering on Alyssa's face. OK, so her own panic reactions were about to ruin her daughter's whole experience. Summer couldn't help the panic. It was a given in her life now. Always on caution. But to deprive Alyssa because of her problems? She couldn't do that. Wouldn't do that. "But, yes, a few samples would be good. Thank you."

"Chris is really into the chocolate chocolate," Rick suggested from behind her.

Standing so close to her, his voice practically in her ear… Summer startled again. Sucked in a sharp breath, held it until the panic passed, then let it out. "Chocolate chocolate's fine," she said, then also picked out one sample of strawberry, and one of mint chocolate chip for her daughter.

"You're really not going to have anything?" Rick asked her. "I mean, look at all these flavors. Bubble-gum surprise, blue goo, mystery chunks… They all sound pretty tempting to me."

She reached over and took a mini spoon of chocolate chocolate from the counter boy, handed it to Alyssa, then turned to Rick. "Maybe they tempt you, but they scare me. Blue goo, for example. What, exactly, goes into ice cream that turns it blue? And I don't even want to think about the goo part."

"Then have vanilla. It's safe. No surprises. Not particularly imaginative, but very good for the soul in its dependability."

She took another sample and handed it to Alyssa. Actually, dependability for the soul was everything she wanted in her life…in her world. And it had nothing to do with vanilla ice cream

"The soul?"

"Any ice cream is good for the soul."

"Just how do you figure that?"

"It makes you feel good. Makes you happy. Puts a smile on your face."

Exactly what she needed but couldn't have for more than moments at a time. Summer did smile for one of those moments, though, thinking about that life, thinking about how hard Rick was working to make her happy right then. She didn't smile often, but she really appreciated his enthusiasm. More than that, she was flattered by the way he was trying so hard to make this a nice experience for her. Nobody, other than Grace Corbett, had done that for her in a very long time.

"See, I'm right. You're smiling already. And you haven't even eaten any ice cream."

"Maybe I'm not hungry," she said, taking the third mini-spoon and handing it to Alyssa.

"But eating ice cream isn't about being hungry. It's about…relaxing. Kicking back, letting the day's troubles go, even if for only a little while. Enjoying a simple pleasure."

As if she could. "So, what if I raise the calorie argument? Tell you that I'm watching my weight." Which wasn't true. If anything, it was a struggle to keep weight on these days, thanks to the stress. "Will you quit trying to force feed me ice cream then?"

Rick moved backwards a step, then took a long deliberate look at her, toe to head and back again. "Trust me…and this is strictly a professional medical opinion…you don't have any worries in the weight department. Besides…" he pointed to the five-gallon tub at the end of the display "…sugar-free, low-fat."

In spite of herself, Summer's smile bubbled into laughter. It was a simple thing, really. Go with the moment. Have a scoop of ice cream.

Enjoy herself. "OK, so maybe one scoop…blue goo, though. Not vanilla. It's so…ordinary."

"So the lady really knows how to cut loose," Rick commented, then stepped forward to order the rest of the ice cream…chocolate chocolate all the way around, except for the blue goo. "Extra sprinkles for everybody," he said. "And, Chris, why don't you and Alyssa go play in Kiddieland while we wait?"

"Kiddieland?" A knot of panic rose up in Summer again as she looked across the parlor at the sectioned-off area for children. It was full of games and toys, little penny rides in the form of horses and dinosaurs, and small tables meant for the kids to enjoy their treats without the parents breathing down their necks. A perfect place for children, as a matter of fact. And it scared her to death. "Um, Alyssa and I don't really have time to—" Before her words were out, Alyssa had broken free of Summer's hand once more and scampered off with Chris.

"It's really very safe," Rick said.

"I, um…" There was no explaining this away. She was an over-protective parent. Alyssa grew up in a very guarded world. That was just the way it was. "I'm worried about the germs," she lied.

"There's not anything there she won't be exposed to anywhere else. And Tom Benson is fastidious about cleaning everything every day. Sometimes several times a day." He paused, contemplated her for a moment. "Are you OK, Summer? You look…nervous."

She was. And she was embarrassed it showed so much. "We live a quiet life. I probably go a little overboard with Alyssa, but she's all I have in the world." Not really a good explanation, but good enough.

"Well, I do understand that," he said, taking two of the ice-cream cones and handing them to Summer. "Chris is all I have, and I treasure my time with him. Maybe go overboard myself, spoiling him a little, probably trying to compensate, or even overcompensate, in some ways, for his not having a mother around."

That much was true. Over-protecting, over-compensating…it was what she did, who she was. Or who she'd turned into. There was nothing in her parenting that happened by chance. Not even by trial and error. For her, every bit of it was a well-planned daily existence. "Whatever works," she said, following Rick across the room to the table that sat square in the middle of the front window. Table with a view, overlooking main street. Best one in the house. But not the one Summer wanted. So, while Rick took ice cream cones to the children, she moved to a more secluded table in the corner, and took the seat with the best view of Kiddieland.

"He's a really good father," Julie Corbett said, stepping up to Summer. Julie had her niece, Molly Corbett, in tow. "I knew Rick when we were kids, would have never pictured him this way. But he does it right."

Summer turned and smiled at Julie, who was married to Jess Corbett, one of the two owners of Lilly Lake Hospital. She and Julie worked together as nurses occasionally, as well as shared the same love for the abandoned and abused horses taken in and cared for by the Gracie Foundation. "How's Edie feeling? I saw Rafe a couple of days ago and he said she's ready to... well, his exact word was pop." She laughed. "I remember that stage with Alyssa, where all I wanted to do was go into labor, get it over with, and move on into the next step of being a mother. For me, that's when time really dragged out." She was referring to Edie Corbett, who was married to the hospital's other owner, Rafe, brother to Jess.

"Well, that's what Edie's going through right now. She's ready to deliver any minute and getting pretty anxious about it since, technically, she's a week overdue. Which is why I've got Molly for the day. Molly was being pretty rambunctious, and I thought Rafe and Edie could use some alone time before the blessed event…time without having to worry about Molly. Besides, after the new baby is born, that's not going to happen again for a while. So I thought this would be good for them. Especially for Edie, since Rafe's all into pampering her right now."

What a wonderful thought, spending those last moments before birth with the father of your child…the man you *loved*. She hadn't had that. Hadn't had anything even close to that. "I'm sure they appreciate it," she said, sounding wistful.

"Aunt Julie, can I go play with Chris and Alyssa?" Molly asked, tugging at Julie's hand.

Julie let go of her niece immediately, allowing her to scramble over to Kiddieland. "What kind of ice cream do you want?" she called after her.

"Chocolate," Molly called back.

"The flavor of the day is chocolate chocolate, with extra sprinkles," Summer said, her gaze fixed on the children. Taking quick peeks at Rick, though, when he wasn't paying attention.

"And look at you, eating blue."

"Yes, just look at me, eating blue." She sighed, finally relaxing back into her chair. All in all, this whole *ordeal* was only a little thing. But sometimes those little things counted. If the expression on her daughter's face right now meant anything, this impromptu trip to the ice-cream parlor was counting for a whole lot. Alyssa was glowing, playing with her friends. Having the time of her life. "Blue, with sprinkles."

"Well, I think they're all settled in for a few minutes," Rick said, returning to the table, not mentioning a word about Summer's table switch. Holding out a chair for Julie, he asked, "Care to join us?"

"I'd like to but I've got some phone calls to make. I thought I'd go sit in the other corner and work for a few minutes while Molly plays. With the ER expansion under way now, I've got a lot of new equipment to look at, more sales reps to talk to than I ever thought I'd have to deal with, and not enough hours in the day to get it all done." She held up her cellphone. "So, work goes with me, even to Benson's Ice Creamery. I appreciate the offer, but duty calls." With that, she headed to the back corner of the parlor and sat down.

"She's dedicated," Rick said. "We're lucky she decided to come back to Lilly Lake once she finished her education, because she's got amazing talent as a nurse and also as an administrator."

"She said you two go back a long time." Somehow, she felt a little envious. Nobody in her life went back very far.

"We were kids. Ran around together for a while. Got into trouble a couple times."

"Like boyfriend and girlfriend?" OK, that was none of her business, but she was curious.

He shook his head. "Nope. More like allies. Julie was one of Grace Corbett's foster-children, and I was the son of Lawrence Corbett's maid. We both felt a little left out or excluded from certain things. Gave us a common bond." Thinking back, he grinned. "Or a common goal to raise a little hell wherever we could."

Summer knew what feeling excluded felt like. These days, she felt it acutely herself. "Well, whatever kind of past she had, she's certainly a talented woman…in her nursing skills, in her ability with horses."

"You're not bad with the horses yourself. And as a nurse, I'd rank you right up there with Julie. Speaking of nursing…"

As a nurse…she didn't want to get into that issue right here. She and Rick had gone round and round before, and nothing had changed. She wasn't going to take the full-time position he'd been offering her. So she quickly scuttled that part of conversation and turned it around to horses…safe territory. "Grace gave me that experience with horses. I love animals…all animals. Hadn't ever been around horses, though. Didn't grow up in a situation where anything like horseback riding was available to me. So when I moved into Gracie House to take care of her, she offered me the opportunity to do something I'd always wanted to do…learn to ride. And I loved it. Loved her for giving it to me." A faint smile slipped to her lips, remembering that first day Grace had taken her down to the stables. She'd found Jasmine right off, a shy, gentle chestnut. Had fallen in love with her. A week later, Grace had given her Jasmine. "I really miss her," she said fondly.

"So do I. Grace touched a lot of lives. Mine included, when she endowed me to go to medical school."

"She did that for you?"

Rick nodded. "At the time, I didn't even know I wanted to be a doctor. I was in college, not majoring in anything. Kind of on the verge of washing out, actually." He smiled. "Let me rephrase that. I was being a real screw-up. Mad at my mother, mad at the world in general. On academic probation, on disciplinary probation. Probably days away from being kicked to the curb. Then one day, Grace showed up at my dorm room, walked right in and made me an offer. Get my act together, start taking pre-med classes to see if I liked medicine. If I did, she'd send me to medical school." He didn't talk about himself much. No reason to. People here either remembered him as a kid and held onto their prejudices or accepted what he'd become, or they'd come to know him as an adult only and based their opinion on what they saw. He did his job, raised his kid, kept to himself. That was his world, and that was all he wanted in his world. But something about Summer compelled him to be, well, a little more loquacious than he normally was. In fact, Summer was the first person he'd ever told about Grace making his medical education available to him. He wasn't even sure Rafe and Jess knew, and didn't feel inclined to mention it to them.

"So, just like that, you changed your life?"

He shook his head. "Not really. I gave it some thought. Didn't like the idea of all the years of study I'd have ahead of me. I wasn't very focused then so I turned her down. In due course, I grew up some, and got a little more serious about my studies…at least, enough so I wasn't in imminent danger of getting myself kicked out. Then about a year later I went home on semester break and she offered me a one-week job at the hospital. Hard work, no pay, was what she said." He chuckled. "I'd always had free access to the stables and the horses. She told me for *that* door to remain open during my holiday, I had to work that week at the hospital in exchange for my privileges. No hospital, no horses. So I took on the hospital. Did grunt work, nothing glamorous. It nearly broke my back. In fact, I was so tired I never rode once during that week. But after one particularly rough night, where I actually assisted in a resuscitation…I was the one to do the chest compressions that helped save the patient's life…let's say that my life changed. It was the first time I'd ever done anything I considered worthwhile, and I floated around on a high from that for weeks. *I saved a life.* The rest is history, and here I am. Thank God for Grace Corbett and her phenomenal insight into people."

"I wish I'd known her longer, but she…" Summer paused, drew in a ragged breath. "Taking care of her all those months when she was dying, it was never like I was really working. It was more like being part of something important. And she was so good to Alyssa… I didn't know Grace as long as everybody else around here did, but I don't think I've ever re-spected anybody more in my life."

"She was one of the truly good people." He licked his ice-cream cone, then pointed to the blue melting down the side of Summer's cone. "You'd better get after that blue stuff fast," he said, handing her a napkin. "And in the mean-time, while I've got you distracted, I'm going to make that offer again."

Summer shook her head. "No, Rick. Don't do it, because I haven't changed my mind. I like my working situation as it is. Being a temp nurse is…good." Kept her largely unnoticed, off to the side, which was exactly where she wanted to be these days. She raised her daughter, she worked occasionally. It was enough. Although she did have to admit that she missed full-time involve-ment. Missed the financial security, too. Maybe again someday…

"But it doesn't pay you as much as you could earn coming on staff as a full-time RN, and you're a damned good nurse, Summer. I wouldn't be asking you to head the pediatric ward if I hadn't already seen how you work. The hospi-tal needs you and I think you need the hospital."

"See, that's the thing. I *don't* need the hospital. At least, not in the capacity you're offering me. Coming in occasionally, working wherever I'm needed…that's all I want to do." She glanced over at Alyssa, then back at Rick. "I value my time with my daughter, and a full-time job would take too much of that away from me."

"Like my job as chief of staff takes too much time away from me. But I make it work, Summer. Sometimes I don't like all the hours I have to put in, but at the end of the day, it works out."

"I'm glad it does. But I can't do it."

This was the third time he'd offered her this position, and had been turned down that many times. Yet he still wanted her in that job. Hadn't even considered looking for someone else yet. Summer was a good nurse. No, she was great. She had the right instincts as well as a natural gift with children. Maybe her greatest ability was the way she put people at ease. As far as he was concerned, she was the only person he wanted, and he wasn't going to be deterred by what he was sure was going to be his next rejection. "Look, I don't know what's stopping you. If it's someone reliable to look after Alyssa, bring her to my house. Mrs. Jenkins is there looking after Chris, and—"

Summer thrust out her hand to stop him. "That's not the point, Rick. I…I can't get that involved right now. Not with anything."

"What if I sweetened the pot by telling you that we're going to start a day-care program for employees' children? Alyssa could be included in that program, and you'd get to be with her throughout the day. So, would that be enough to make you consider accepting?"

She hesitated. Narrowed her eyes. Didn't refuse right away, which gave him his first glimmer of hope.

"It does make it more intriguing," she admitted.

Finally, he was making headway. Letting his hopes rise just a little bit.

"But not enough to accept the offer. I'm sorry, Rick. I can't do it."

Hopes dashed to pieces again. But he'd almost hooked her, which meant he wasn't giving up. Summer was odd, though. Intriguing. Beautiful, with her long blonde hair, her ocean-blue eyes. And she was frustrating as hell. He wanted her, and the more she refused, the more he wanted her. "Well, I'm not giving up. You're the right person for the position, and I'm pretty damned stubborn."

"So am I," she said, smiling. "If you still want me to temp, and I hope you do, I'll be glad to do that occasionally. But I don't want…responsibility. Not the kind you're offering me."

Yet when she stepped into a position, even a temporary one, she assumed the responsibility like nobody he'd ever seen. It was her nature. The people around her looked to her for leadership. Unfortunately, this was not an argument to wage today. There would be no giving up on her, though. There would be other days, other opportunities, other trips to Benson's Ice Creamery, he hoped as he watched the children playing together. Watched with pride as his son stood right up for Alyssa, showed her the so-called ropes of Kiddieland.

Summer saw the children's relationship going on. In fact, she was paying more attention to the children than she was to him which was, admittedly, a little bit of a blow to the ego. Even though he wasn't interested in Summer *that way.* But to get upstaged by the children? He could feel the slight sting of it. "Of course I still want you as a temp. But this isn't over, Summer. Not by a long shot." In fact, for a moment the thought of a real date with her passed before his eyes. He had to blink pretty hard to get rid of it, though. Because that wouldn't work. He didn't have time. He didn't want the drama either, and one way or another those kinds of relationships always led to drama. For this part of his life, he was dad first, then doctor after that. That's all. "So I'm warning you…"

Summer laughed, but kept her eyes focused on the children. "You got your way with the blue goo. What more do you want?"

What more did he want? The sun, the moon, and Summer Adair. His hospital needed her, and what was good for the hospital was good for him. So now all he had to do was find a way to convince Summer she needed what he wanted.

As it had turned out, the evening had been nice. Rick was very good company in spite of how he'd pestered her again about the pediatric job. Alyssa had certainly enjoyed playing with Chris.

Then, on top of all that, *sprinkles* became the most important thing in her daughter's life. She'd asked if she could have them on her breakfast cereal in the morning and on her peanut-butter sandwich for tomorrow's lunch.

It was her daughter's horizons broadening. Made Summer proud, scared her, too, as it changed their direction. Turned one step forward into something a little unsure simply because Alyssa had asserted herself today. Under other circumstances, Summer would have been excited about that. But under *these* circumstances, her real inclination was to pull her daughter closer, protect her a little more.

In a sense, Summer did feel guilty sheltering her daughter the way she did. When they'd lived with Grace she'd had Molly to play with. Still did, whenever she took Alyssa up to Gracie House for either Edie or Mrs. Murdock, the housekeeper, to watch. And now Chris Navarro was in her life. So Alyssa's world was definitely expanding. But was that enough for her? Summer did worry about that. Worried about Alyssa picking up *her* anxieties, too.

"So maybe taking that job at the hospital and

giving Alyssa the chance to interact with all the children in the day-care center would be a good thing," she said to Clancy. He was the huge orange tomcat that had adopted them when they'd moved into the cottage. Apparently, he'd called it home for quite a while before she and Alyssa had arrived, and had no problem at all sharing it, especially with people who fed him on a regular basis. A gentle soul, really, he snuggled into Summer's side when she plopped down on the sofa and picked up a medical journal to read. "She just lights up around other children," she continued to the cat. "Loved playing with Molly and Chris this evening. So tell me, Clancy. Am I being too over-protective? I mean, this is Lilly Lake, New York. It's safe here. Out of the way. Who's going to come here looking for me?"

Who, indeed. Maybe an ex-husband? A thought that chilled her to the bone. Only thing was, thinking about the job Rick had offered warmed her. So did the image of Rick that popped into her mind.

"Besides, I'd really love to work again. Have a permanent position. And Rick's offer..." She scratched Clancy behind the ears, eliciting his purr. "Sure, life is easy for you. You have some-one to take care of you. Don't have to worry about anything because it's all being provided for you, you lucky cat."

In a sense, though, Grace had done the same for her. And it was Grace on her mind when she picked up the phone quite a while later and dialed Rick Navarro's cellphone.

"Hello," he said, his voice thick.

"Hi, Rick. It's Summer. Did I wake you?" She glanced at the clock, surprised to see that it was well after eleven.

He cleared his throat before he answered. "You're not craving more blue goo, are you?"

He always did that, always made her smile. "What I'm craving is a meeting in the morning. One where we discuss the terms of my new job."

"Well, that was definitely worth waking up for," he said, suddenly sounding alert.

The thing was, she was having quite the op-posite reaction. Now that she'd committed her-self, all she wanted to do was go curl up for a nice, cozy sleep. Something she hadn't done since she couldn't remember when. Normally, her sleep was rigid, interrupted, unrestful. But something about her decision, something about hearing Rick's voice the last thing in her day… definitely a good night's sleep ahead.

CHAPTER TWO

"IT's a pretty straightforward idea, Summer. We want to expand the pediatric department, integrate more kinds of medical services, especially rehabilitation." Rick pushed a rough-up of the floor plan across the desk to Summer. "We've got the space allotted, and the architects are working on some ideas to maximize the space we already have so they can integrate that into the new space we're going to build. In total, we're going to double the square footage and bring in an additional five services we haven't offered before. In size, this expansion equals what we're doing in trauma, and it's going to give us the largest pediatric service in the region."

She studied the plan for a moment, liked what she saw. Lilly Lake Hospital, as it operated now, had a tidy little pediatric department that offered the basics. It was good already, but what Rick had in mind was going to make it great. Being part of it excited her. More than that, it revived the passion she'd once felt for medicine, passion she'd lost during her marriage and had never recovered. Now she could feel the tingle. But she had to keep it reined in until she was actually hired, and Rick did still have to go over her credentials. That made her nervous. They were solid, no faking her background, but would they be enough for him now that she was under the microscope, so to speak? "I've never run an entire department. Just an intensive care unit. Is that good enough for you?"

"Grace found you and hired you, so that's good enough for me."

"And the day-care unit?"

"Maybe not a top priority, but we can get it launched in a small capacity almost immediately."

It was sounding more and more appealing.

"So, what aren't you telling me?" There was always a catch, wasn't there? That little hidden bit of information that didn't come out until after the fact. Like a husband who enjoyed beating his wife but hadn't shown the proclivity until after they were married.

"Nothing that I can think of."

She looked hard into Rick's eyes, studied them for a moment, then nodded. "OK, then…" She saw no guile there. Saw no mean spirit. "With the provision that there will be a day-care program, I'll take the job." And just like that, she was committed. Also excited.

"Done deal, then."

"That's too easy," she quipped.

"It was meant to be. I realized somewhere between your second and third refusal that we had to figure your daughter into the equation. I have a great housekeeper and nanny looking after Chris, but if I didn't, I'd want him here, with me. So I put myself in your position and saw that someone to care for Alyssa was probably the only thing stopping you from accepting."

"That's being overly optimistic, don't you think?" Or extremely observant.

"Maybe. But the gamble paid off, didn't it? I've done the preliminary work toward getting the day-care center off the ground, and you've accepted the job."

"I'm not really that easy," she said, feeling flattered, and a little awkward about how well he could anticipate her.

"Not easy at all. You've caused me to lose sleep, Summer."

"Let me guess. You lay awake at night, trying to figure out what it would take to persuade me to accept the position. Right?"

He grinned. "Something like that."

"Well, then…" She stood, not sure what else to do at this point. "I'll start tomorrow."

"Tomorrow. Oh, and day care will be open. I hired someone to watch the children until we're fully functional and have a real staff in place."

"Qualified?"

"Eminently. She was my third-grade teacher. Retired now. I've put her in charge, temporarily, with the option of staying on to head the program, if she's as good as I think she'll be."

A new job, a place where Alyssa would be safe… Just like that, her life had changed yet again. But it was a good change. This time. At least, that's what she kept telling herself all the way home.

* * *

Jess Corbett plopped down in the chair across the desk from Rick. "You look like you just opened a whole bunch of Christmas presents," he said, smiling. "All of them good."

"In a way, I did," Rick said. "Summer's finally consented to being head nurse in Pediatrics."

"Well. I'll be damned. It only took you, what? Three months? Julie said she wasn't sure Summer would ever do it, but I figured if you wanted her bad enough, you'd figure out a way to get her. So, what did it take?" Jess stretched out his long legs and leaned back in the chair, cupping his hands behind his head. "And is this going to be a long story? Because I've got to go see a patient on my way out, go home and have breakfast with my lovely wife, then teach a class on CPR."

Rick was beginning to like Jess. Not completely there yet, but working on it and trying hard to get over that last hurdle of trust. They had history, most of it pretty bad. Jess and his older brother, Rafe, had been the bullies, and he their favorite victim, when they were kids. Kids' stuff, most of it, but pretty hurtful at times, since his mother's livelihood had depended on their father employing her. Which meant he himself had had to sit back and take it. And they had known how to dish it out, Rafe physically, Jess verbally, all of it owing to the abuse they'd suffered at the hands of their father. When he'd been a kid, Rick hadn't known the whole psychological profile of how abuses often begat abuses. All he'd known had been that Rafe and Jess had come at him whenever they'd had a chance, and he'd hated them for it.

Well, it was all in the past now. They were adults. Rafe and Jess had apologized many times over. More than that, their earnestness came through in their actions toward Rick. They owned the hospital, but had turned it over to him to run the medical aspects of it. More than that, he had equal weight in all the decisions. They treated him fairly. "Not so long as it is complicated. And it only took me two months, not three."

Jess chuckled. "Isn't that always the way when a beautiful woman's involved? I mean, look what happened to me when I got involved with my beautiful woman. All the things I swore I'd never do...well, I'm doing them. And I'm very happy with my life since I met Julie. So tell me, what's your beautiful lady got you caught up in?"

Rick shook his head, conjuring up a quick flash of Summer when she'd flounced out his door. And flouncing it had been. Or maybe he'd wanted her to flounce, fantasized her flouncing. Whatever… "Well, she's not mine, not going to be mine. Did that once, and my ex *was* beautiful, but I'm not going to let my head be turned like that again with anybody else. My marriage woes aside, though, this particular beautiful woman wanted a little extra incentive to come and work here."

Jess arched amused eyebrows. "Let me guess. A day-care center for hospital staff? Julie's mentioned that to me a time or two and, so you'll know, she's pretty well lined up with Summer on this one. She wants a day-care program, too, for when we get started on the family situation."

"So you knew this was going to happen?"

"You want Summer. We all want Summer. And Summer's all about her little girl. According to Julie, she has the worst separation anxiety she's ever seen. It's so bad she nearly has panic attacks when Alyssa is out of her sight. Plus, she's got a pretty short list of people she trusts to watch Alyssa when she's working. So, yes, I figured it was going to happen sooner or later. You know, give a little, get a lot."

"But it's a good move for the entire staff, too," Rick explained. "Not just Summer, and not just *for* Summer. As we expand our services, we'll be bringing in more people to work. To get the best-qualified people we can, we've got to offer them the perks that other hospitals our size don't. Salary and nice facilities aside, it has to be about the human touch...our day-care program, for starters. Then other quality-of-life issues. And before you tell me this is something I should have discussed with you and Rafe..."

Jess thrust out his hand to stop him. "Your decision, Rick. If you think we need it, then we'll do it. You don't need our permission to dot every 'i' and cross every 't'. OK? And for what it's worth, I'm with you on it. Rafe will be too, although he's probably too tied up with Edie right now to care about much of anything going on around here. He's taking these last days of pregnancy much harder than his wife is. But he'll be behind you when he's not so distracted, because he'll understand the benefits of this, too."

You don't need our permission... That was the part of his job he was still getting used to, the part where he had all the authority. The Rafe and Jess Corbett he'd spent half his growing-up years fighting and hating trusted him implicitly with their hospital. They'd even mentioned bringing him on as a full partner at some point, an idea he couldn't quite wrap his psyche around because sometimes it still felt like he was treading on eggshells, waiting for them to resort to their old selves. *They* were the ones who were past all that, though. Which made his trust issues entirely *his* problem as there were still days when he woke up wondering if this would be the day they pulled the rug out from under him.

"Well, I'm glad you're good with this because Summer's going to start tomorrow, and our new day-care programs starts tomorrow, too. Anita Johnson will head it up to begin with and with any luck maybe permanently. Remember her?"

Jess arched his eyebrows. "I'm impressed. She was probably one of the best school teachers I ever knew. But I thought she was retired."

"Retired, and bored. So I thought who better than to take care of the kids *of* the kids she taught?"

"You cover all the angles, don't you?" Jess asked, chuckling.

"As many as I have to."

"Good. I'm glad we're moving forward. Aunt Grace put her trust in the right man when she hired you." He stood. "Anyway, like I said, I've got to teach a class in two hours, and I've got a lot to do before that." Jess was a part-time trauma surgeon as well as paramedic trainer and second in charge of the Lilly Lake Volunteer Fire Department, walking the line between the two careers. One of those rare individuals who could do it all.

"How's the program coming?" Rick asked, referring to the paramedic training that was actually a hospital and fire department cross-over program.

"Got three people in it right now. Give us a few months and I think we're going to have a good team in place and an even better training program going into our next round. I've got about a dozen people interested in taking the upcoming class. A few of them coming in from other towns."

Times were changing in Lilly Lake, Rick thought as Jess headed out. Suddenly, he was excited. The times really were changing, and he was cautiously optimistic. And smiling. Although that smile had more to do with Summer than anything else.

"Oh, my," Summer said, placing a pillow behind Edie Corbett's back. "I think you've doubled in size since I saw you...when was it? Day before yesterday?"

"Not doubled. Tripled. At least, that's what it feels like." She sank back into the pillows on the couch and very gingerly lifted her feet. "You know I've been pregnant for two and a half years, don't you?"

Laughing, Summer sat down in the chair across from her. "My last month carrying Alyssa was miserable. Everything was swollen, including my fingernails. And it felt like there were forty-eight days that month, thirty-six hours in each and every day."

"Well, if nothing happens in the next couple of days, they're going to induce labor."

"But everything's OK, isn't it?" Summer asked.

Edie nodded, grimaced, then smiled. "Everything but my mood. I'm being grumpy. That's why Rafe took the girls down to the stables. He told me I could use some alone time. Loosely translated to mean he needed to get out of the house and Molly needed a break from my last few days of jitters."

"Is Alyssa going to ride?" Summer asked, growing concerned with the idea.

"Rafe promised to put her up on a pony. Molly wanted to give her a tandem saddle and the three of them go up to Hideaway Bluff, but Rafe's pretty cautious when it comes to putting the kids on the horses. So right now they're out in the smaller paddock, going round in circles, and Alyssa's riding with Rafe until he thinks she's safe to do tandem."

Gracie House, and the whole estate, was one of the few places she actually felt safe. And knowing that Alyssa was with Rafe didn't bother her as much as it might have at one time because

Gracie House was home. Even though she didn't live in it now, the safety she'd felt when she had still seeped in. It was always good to come back. Although, in reality, she still lived on the property, not even half a mile away. "Well, since she's having a good time and I don't want to take that away from her, I suppose I could come back for her later on. Or maybe Rafe could drop her by the house when they've finished."

"Or, you could relax and have tea with me. And I'll promise not to be too grumpy while we wait."

"Are you sure you wouldn't rather take a nap? You're about to give up any hope of sleeping for the next few months."

"Except I've got Rafe. Half the sleep deprivation is going to be his, since this is his endeavor, too." She patted her belly. Grimaced yet again, this time reaching around to massage the small of her back.

"You're lucky. I spent my first few months learning to sleep anywhere, any time I could." Because she hadn't had a husband who would help. In fact, the couple of times when she'd asked for it, he'd either stormed out, which had been preferable, or he'd—

"You did it alone?" Edie cut in, interrupting Summer's thoughts.

Summer nodded. Didn't volunteer any more information.

"I guess I didn't know that. For some reason, I thought you were still married when Alyssa was born."

"In name," she said, wishing the topic had never come up. She didn't talk about it. Not to anyone. Not ever. Oh, Grace had known how bad her marriage had been, but that was different. And while she trusted Edie, silence on the topic of her marriage was still the best thing. Battered wives didn't make for great conversation. In fact, the topic had a way of stopping the conversation cold. "Look, I'm going to go make us that pot of tea. Think happy baby thoughts or take a nap… I'll be back in a minute." With that, she practically jumped off the chair and sprinted to the kitchen, only too glad to get away from the subject.

Slumping against the fridge for support, with the one and only purpose of steadying her nerves, Summer shut her eyes, drew in a deep breath… *New direction. New life.* That's what she had to keep telling herself.

"You OK, Summer?" Myra Murdock, the Corbett housekeeper, asked.

"Fighting off a headache," Summer lied, pushing herself away from the fridge. "Um…what kind of tea does Edie prefer?"

"These days it's green because it's a little lower in caffeine. One cup a day is all she gets, though." Myra pointed to a tin on the counter top. "She likes it with cream. Oh, and help yourself to anything you want. There's a tea caddy in the pantry…the Ceylon is my favorite."

"Ceylon," Summer repeated, as her pulse finally settled down to a normal rhythm.

"Could I ask you for a favor, Summer?" Myra continued. "Since you're going to be staying for tea, would you mind looking after Edie while I run to the post office to mail a package to my granddaughter? Her birthday's next week. I was going to wait until Rafe came back to the house, but if I hurry, the package may still go out today."

"Go," Summer said. "And don't rush. As often

as you've watched Alyssa for me, it's the least I can do."

Tea made, Summer carried it back to the living room, where Edie was trying to readjust her back pillow. "Can't get comfortable," she said, clearly agitated. "No matter which way I turn it, I still get back spasms…"

"Back spasms?" Summer asked, setting down the tea tray. "How long have you been getting them?"

"Most of the day. They're not bad. Just annoying, because every time I get comfortable, I have another one." Edie flinched. "Just like that."

"When Rafe went down to the paddock with the girls, did he know you were having back spasms?" She pulled her cellphone from her pocket.

"I didn't tell him. He's been saint with me, and I've been complaining about so many things lately, I thought he needed the time away. And like I said, they're more an annoyance than anything else."

Summer glanced at her watch, then punched in a number, waited for a ring, and heard it coming from the table next to the front door. Rafe had left his phone behind. "Well, ready or not, I think you're going to have a baby in a little while," she said, punching in another number. "You're probably having back labor," she said, as the ringer on the other end kicked in.

"It's only little twinges." Edie protested. "Labor's supposed to be…painful. These are just…" Another twinge hit, and she readjusted herself on the sofa. "It really couldn't be labor, could it?" she said a moment later.

"Well, I've been timing your twinges, and they're coming pretty regularly, and less than a minute apart," Summer said. "Hey, Rick," she said when he picked up on the other end. "I'm at Gracie House. Edie's contractions are less than a minute apart, Rafe's down at the paddock with the girls… Oh, and his phone is here. So, is Jess still there? I saw him heading down the hall on my way out earlier."

"He's on duty at the firehouse," Rick said. "And we got word they're out on a run, about halfway over to Jasper. Car wreck, minor injuries."

Now she was getting concerned. "And the ambulance is tied up at the wreck?"

"On its way back in with a patient."

"Well, I don't think I can get Edie into my car…" She glanced down at Edie, who was already well into another of her "twinges". "So, with the rate she's speeding up here, and given the fact that this has been in progress for several hours now, this could be a home birth. And unless I miss my guess, she's ready to push."

"Ever done a home birth?"

"No, but I assisted in a few births when I was a student, and did one on my own. *One*, Rick. That's all." She desperately wished Rick was there. Or Rafe. Or Jess. Truth was, in trying to keep up a calm facade for Edie's sake, she was turning into a quivering heap of nerves inside. Delivering babies wasn't her thing. She loved taking care of them, but had never really gained much experience helping them into the world. Other than that one delivery done as a nurse, and having Alyssa, she was totally inexperienced in this.

"Um, Summer…" Edie said. "I think maybe you're right about me needing to push. I'm beginning to feel a lot of pressure…" This time the grimace came with a groan.

Well, this was going to be her third time. So, what was it they said about the third time being a charm? She was keeping her fingers crossed that would be the case. "Look, Rick, I need to go find some towels…" She turned away from Edie. "Real fast," she whispered. "Edie's labor has done a major acceleration, and this baby is fighting to get out. As in right now!"

"Towels are in the laundry room, off the kitchen," Edie panted.

She turned around, nodded at Edie, then broke into a dead run, talking to Rick on the way. "So I need someone here as fast as you can get them. Someone more experienced at this than I am. And see if you can find someone to go get Rafe. He should be here for this, too. Oh, and don't hang up on me, Rick," she said, grabbing an armload of freshly laundered towels and running back to Edie. "I need someone to talk me through it. The last time I even went near a birthing, other than Alyssa, was ten years ago."

"Ten years? Then you should be good to go," he teased.

"Easy for you to say," she quipped, then dropped the load of towels down next to Edie.

Edie began to pant. "Are we going to do this right…?" Another twinge, this time much harder than the others.

"Rick is sending help," Summer said, then clicked the phone over to speaker and set it aside. "In the meantime, I need to take a look to see what's going on. So if you don't mind…"

Edie not only didn't mind, she squirmed herself into the position as fast as she could.

"Help is on the way," Rick's voice cracked out on the wobbly phone connection. "Ten minutes…sooner… I'll be…."

Rick was coming? Was that what he was trying to tell her? Somehow, Summer felt better already. "OK, Edie," she said, removing the shade from the lamp sitting on the table next to the sofa. "Let's see what's happening."

One look told her everything. Edie was fully dilated. Ready to crown. And one feel to Edie's abdomen confirmed it all. "So, are you ready to be a mother?" she asked. "Because we've got a little work to do now." Summer had to remember that even though Edie held an important position at the hospital, she wasn't considered medical staff and hadn't had medical training outside some basic first-aid skills. Her position, as Child Life Specialist, was more about stepping in as the go-between, the person who helped the child through the whole hospital experience, explained the procedures in the way a child could understand them. "I know you feel like pushing, and we'll get to that in just a minute. But I'd like to wait as long as we can, since…"

"No waiting," Edie gasped, grabbing the edge of the couch so hard her knuckles went white. "I want this baby born…*now*!"

"Let me see what I can do." Summer felt Edie's abdomen again, while the next contraction hit, trying to discern the baby's position. "OK, I think your Mary Grace is as impatient as you are, because she's not waiting." Although Summer wanted to wait for Rick, for Rafe, for anybody.

"So give the ladies what they want," Rick said from the phone, sounding almost breathless.

He *was* on his way. Running, she thought. She knew it. More than that, she felt it. Somehow, that made everything feel better, feel right. Rick being on the other end of the phone that was the only reason she was getting through this and appearing reasonably steady. "I think I will. So, let's get you in a little better position. Try sitting up as much as you can. Then draw your knees up. And… I see her! I see your daughter, Edie. At least the top of her. Which means, on your next contraction, go ahead and push."

Edie struggled into place, with Summer's help. Then, winded, she laid her head back on a cushion and shut her eyes for a moment. "Remind me to renew my gym membership. I didn't know I was so out of shape."

"Neither did I when I went through this," Summer said, as she placed a few extra pillows behind Edie's back. "And let me warn you, while it's a beautiful thing, and I'd do it all over again, several more times actually, afterwards I ached for days in places I didn't know could ache. But it's worth it."

"Just get her out," Edie begged. "Just, please, get her out of me!"

Summer took a quick pulse, wishing she had something to monitor fetal progress. So far, this process had taken mere minutes…minutes that seemed like hours. "Rick, I'm going to attempt to lift the baby's head. Anything you want to tell me?"

"Um…good luck?"

Summer laughed. "And for that you got your medical degree?"

"Are you two…?" Edie began, then another contraction hit, and this time she pushed hard. The baby progressed, but not all the way, and Edie fell back into the pillows.

"Next time," Summer said, taking a second to unclench her clenched muscles.

"A couple?" Edie managed.

"What?"

"Are you and Rick together? You seem so in tune… Oh, oh…" Another contraction hit, and at that exact moment the front door finally, literally burst open, Edie screamed the scream of her life, and Mary Grace Corbett made her entry into the world in one grand whoosh.

"She's beautiful," Summer gasped. "Ten fingers, ten toes…" Then she handed Rafe's daughter over to Rafe, who was standing shoulder to shoulder with Rick, and collapsed on the floor, a bundle of nerves, a flood of *happy* tears. With some very gentle arms wrapped around her.

"You did it," Rick said, holding onto her, rocking her like she was a child to be protected. "Summer, you did it all by yourself!"

She glanced up at Mary Grace as the next wave of medical workers hurried in to whisk mother and daughter off to the hospital. "I did," she said, her voice barely above a whisper. Laying her head against Rick's chest, glad to be there, glad for the support, she drew in a deep breath. Smiled. This was a nice place to be. All of it. Everything. A very nice place to be.

CHAPTER THREE

"SHE'S beautiful," Summer murmured, looking through the nursery window at Mary Grace, who was swaddled in a pink baby blanket and sleeping peacefully. The nostalgia was overwhelming Summer. She truly had never thought about having another baby, but looking at the one she'd helped into the world was doubling her maternal instincts. Another baby girl, or a boy, for her to hold in her arms would be wonderful. A perfect dream. Maybe someday... If, and only if, her life ever got straightened out.

"For someone who's delivered only one baby by herself, you did a good job," Rick said. "Actually, you did a great job. You've got exceptional instincts, picking up on Edie's labor when Edie didn't even know she was in labor, let alone how far along into it she was."

"Labor is different for everybody. If you're expecting pain, and you don't get it, I can see how you wouldn't recognize what those little twinges were, like Edie was having."

"Well, it's a good thing you were there, and did see the situation for what it was."

Summer turned around, with her back to the glass, and leaned. Felt exhausted, which didn't matter. Looked a mess, which did, because she didn't want Rick seeing her like this. Sure, they'd logged time together in the stables, grooming horses, cleaning up messes. But that was different. They'd been in it together. He'd looked as bad as she did. Here, though…she really wanted to look better. Probably her new position as Nursing Supervisor in Pediatrics finally making its mark. "You know what? I need to go home, clean up…spend some time with Alyssa. She wants to hear all about the baby, and I promised her we'd make spaghetti for dinner. So I have to run to the grocery store to pick up a few things for the sauce."

"Home-made sauce?" Rick asked, his eyes widening. "You can make that? The only sauce we ever get comes from a jar. You know, open it up, heat it in the microwave."

Summer laughed. "Well, there's that. And

there's the real thing. You know, chopped vegetables, cook down the tomatoes, add lots of garlic, mushrooms, peppers… My grandmother was Italian and she would have fainted at the sight of commercially prepared sauce."

"I don't suppose you make your own pasta, do you?"

She nodded. "It's easy. Even Alyssa knows how to make pasta."

"And now you're putting me to shame," Rick confessed, "because I can't cook if it doesn't come already prepared, in some sort of package. If it weren't for Mrs. Jenkins, I don't think Chris would even know that food can be made from scratch at home. And even then, she's not a great cook. Sticks to basics, but not a master chef by any means."

"Well, I don't suppose Alyssa even knows you can have spaghetti sauce from a jar, or pasta from a box. But, then, I don't go out a lot, so that gives me more time to cook. In a way, it keeps me connected to my grandmother."

"She's gone now?"

Summer nodded. "I'm the only one left, except Alyssa."

"No aunts or uncles or cousins?"

"Too distant to count. Anyway…" She pushed herself off the glass wall, took one final look at the baby, then headed down the hall. Halfway to the door leading to the main foyer she turned back to Rick. "Bring the wine for us. Nothing fancy. And something without high fructose corn syrup or artificial sweetener for the kids."

"For what?" he asked.

"For home-made spaghetti and sauce. If you want to come for dinner."

OK, so that was probably a huge tactical error, inviting him over for dinner. He was her boss, after all, and fraternizing wasn't a good idea. But having adult conversation over a meal was something she didn't get very often. In fact, this would be the first time she'd invited anybody over socially. Of course, if they discussed work, well…that would make it better, or at least seem less personal. She'd drag out her preliminary plans for the day-care center, let the children play together while the adults kicked back, sipped wine and talked about a way to knock out the wall between the storage closet and the waiting area. They'd make it a casual night. Part business, part pleasure.

Suddenly, Summer was excited about the evening ahead. But she wasn't sure if it was about the prospect of moving forward with her new job, sitting across the dinner table with an adult, or because that adult was Rick Navarro. Whatever the case, she fairly floated through the grocery store, picking up various items for the sauce, almost nervous over the prospect of cooking for a man. The last time she'd done that had been... She had to think about it for a moment. These days, she tried blotting out everything she could about Cameron. Tall, handsome, brutal. Ice for a heart. Oh, she'd cooked for him, cleaned for him, serviced him in bed the way a dutiful wife was supposed to. And she'd worked, too, as the head nurse in a pediatric intensive care unit. None of it had been enough, though. No matter what she'd done, no matter how hard she'd tried, it had never been enough. Men like Cameron couldn't be pleased. Not even with her culinary skills, which she knew were good.

Well, no more thinking about that. No way she wanted those memories ruining the evening, and they would, if she wasn't careful. They always did when her resolve wore down and her anxieties reared up. But not tonight. Not when Rick was coming to dinner. But only casually, of course.

"Looks easy enough," Rick commented, gazing over Summer's shoulder. He'd watched her though the process of making the pasta, cooking the tomatoes down to a sauce, chopping up the vegetables. He'd even had a hand in chopping the onions, until Summer had called him off because his pieces had been too large. She was very persnickety about those culinary details. Now she was adding green peppers and getting ready to toss in the mushrooms, all in unmistakably smaller pieces than the onions had been until she'd re-chopped them. "Are you sure you don't want me to do something else…non-vegetable?"

She pointed to the cheese grater sitting on the counter. "Block of Parmesan cheese is in the refrigerator. I like it fresh on the spaghetti, not from a tub or can." Smiling, she turned to face him. "Do you know how to grate cheese?"

He faked rolling up his sleeves. "Let me at it. I'm the best cheese grater you'll ever come across in the entire state of New York."

"I have my doubts," she teased. "In fact, I'm betting you didn't even know Parmesan came in a block."

"Would you be saying that because I botched the onions?" He arched amused eyebrows.

"I'm saying that because you're a man whose idea of a good meal is opening a can of something, or stopping for take-out on his way home from work."

He clutched his chest. "You've hurt me to the very core."

"If you're hurt to the core, it's because of the food you've been eating. But my home-made pasta is guaranteed to cure you…to the very core."

This conversation was getting dangerously close to turning flirtatious, and she was enjoying it way too much. Meaning it was time to stop, take a deep breath, re-group and come back at it from an entirely different angle. "Look, I think it's way too quiet in the other room. Maybe you should go check on the kids?" In other words, get him out of sight, *but quick*, then hopefully he'd be out of mind as well.

Rick gave her a curious look, then backed away. "Maybe I should."

In a matter of seconds she was alone in the kitchen, feeling a little weak in the knees.

Which was stupid. But for a minute there she'd started to feel…secure and snug. Part of something she really shouldn't feel part of. Or maybe the word was happy. In other words, her guard was down, pretty much all the way to the floor. Naturally, it was a mistake she would have to correct, of course, but she enjoyed Rick's company, his conversation. And living in the moment was nice for a change. Too bad she couldn't go there again. Or, at least, not as far as she'd almost gone. Her resolve slowly being restored, Summer returned to chopping vegetables.

Rick stood off to the side of the doorway, unseen to Summer yet watching her. Beautiful, confident in her skills, still trying to stay emotionally detached. She was a puzzle for sure, and while she had a right to be any way she wanted, staying detached didn't suit her. Wasn't her natural personality. He'd worked with her at the hospital, and also at the Gracie Foundation. He'd seen her when she wasn't being so careful or guarded, so he knew what was under that restrained exterior. But that exterior was what she wanted people to see, so he'd respect it. What else could he do?

"The kids are fine," he said, keeping himself well away from her when he finally stepped into the kitchen. "They were playing games, and right now Chris is reading a book to Alyssa. It's about a little bunny that's afraid to come out of its bunny house." Like Summer, who was afraid to come out of herself. When it came right down to it, though, so was he. "And I, um...I want to go back and hear how the story turns out, if you don't mind." Let her have her space, which was clearly what she wanted.

"It's a great ending," she said, her voice unusually reserved, as if she'd tied up her emotions and put them away for safekeeping. "Go, listen to it."

What made Summer tick? He wondered about it as he sat down next to Alyssa on the floor to become part of Chris's audience. In fact, he thought about it so much he missed the ending to the story and had to pick up the book and read it for himself after the kids scampered off to play in the yard. What got the bunny out of the bunny house? It was a simple answer. Someone the bunny trusted.

The thing was, he was pretty sure Summer didn't trust. Same with him, and he knew that. He also knew he shouldn't get involved. As in no more ice cream, no more spaghetti. No more thoughts. Now all he had to do was find a way to go against that deeper urge to connect because damn if he didn't like being with her.

Dinner was casual. They sat on the kitchen floor, balancing plates on their laps. Not because Summer intended to entertain that way, but because the children had ganged up on them about having a picnic. OK, so maybe some people wouldn't agree that the children should get their way, but this was a simple thing. Since it was drizzling outside, Chris and Alyssa wanted to picnic on the floor, and Rick had jumped right into that line. So they spread out a blanket and picnicked in the kitchen, with salads and bread set out in front of them and precariously perched plates of spaghetti. Had she known this was going to turn into a picnic, she would have made sandwiches. But this was actually nice, and kind of funny, watching Rick trying to juggle his plate and get the spaghetti all the way to his mouth without spilling it.

"I think you have a little sauce on your shirt," she said, pointing to a dribble about mid-chest on him.

"No more than you do," he countered.

"So why are we doing this when the kids are already done and back playing games? I mean, shouldn't we be sitting at the table like adults now?"

"We could. But being an adult is highly overrated sometimes. Seeing the world though the eyes of your child is…refreshing." He scooted over next to her, and they sat inches apart, with their backs to the kitchen cabinets. "The bad part about growing up is that we lose every last speck of childhood in the process."

"It would be nice to be able to hang onto some of it when you're an adult, wouldn't it? Alyssa has such amazement for things she's never seen, never experienced. Like the other day. We took a walk down to the lake and there was some sort of bug…a beetle. My reaction to bugs is, well…embarrassing. They scare me, I don't like them. But my daughter knelt down in the dirt and watched that beetle from all angles. Asked me to take pictures of it with my phone. She was fascinated by it, and I kept wondering if I was ever that fascinated by a bug. Or was I just born old and jaded?"

He chuckled. "You're not jaded, and I really can't picture you being old. But I know what you're saying. A couple weeks ago I wandered by the pediatric ward and there was a little girl in the play room, sitting there all alone. She had a game board spread out on a table and she was hoping somebody could come along to play with her. So I walked on by, got halfway down the hall, then went back and spent the next forty-five minutes playing kiddie games. Having real fun. Then I noticed that people were watching me…staff, other patients, parents. They were standing out in the hall, probably whispering about why the chief-of-staff was laughing and enjoying himself playing a game designed for six-year-olds. And I became…embarrassed. It was like they'd discovered my secret, that I still have a bit of the little boy in me, or wanted to, and I didn't want them knowing it."

"So what would they think if they saw us eating dinner on the kitchen floor?"

"Maybe that should be our secret. Don't tell anybody, and they won't have a reason to speculate."

That was her motto, actually. Don't tell. No one would understand. There were times when even she didn't understand why her life had turned out the way it had, why she'd stayed, why she'd...caved in. Tough questions, without answers. And when she thought about them, those were the moments when she truly would have loved being cloaked in childhood innocence again. But there was no going back, was there? Hardly any going forward either. So, for this instant, the kitchen floor was pleasant. No expectations, no explanations. Just floor. "But people always speculate, don't they? That's human nature. If we don't know then we speculate, or assume, based on what we see. Almost from the beginning, my parents told me never to make judgments until I knew the facts. *All the facts.*

They said I could hurt others doing that but more than that I could hurt myself. Limit myself. Then after they were gone…"

"They died?"

She nodded. "When I was a teenager. But I was one of the lucky ones who had a wonderful grandmother… Anyway, she was a little more to the point. She told me that while I'm judging them, they're judging me, and I didn't like that, knowing that people who might not even know me were basing their opinion of me on things they didn't know or understand. The thing is, I do that. Even though I know it's wrong, I do it all the time."

"How did *you* judge me the first time we met?"

Grace had been hosting a small party. She'd only just arrived, hadn't unpacked, looked pretty shabby from a long drive. Then there had been Alyssa, who had been coming down with a cold and grumpy as all get-out. Summer remembered sneaking down the back stairs to the kitchen to see if she could find her daughter some juice, and there Rick had been, standing in the doorway, looking about as uncomfortable as she'd felt. And so…so handsome.

"My impression was that you didn't like parties, and that you didn't fare well in social situations. For that, I judged you favorably because I don't like parties so much, and I certainly don't do well in social situations."

"So you judged me favorably? Or you speculated that I was OK because we had certain characteristics in common?"

She nodded. "I thought you were…" *Sexy.* "Good-natured. Polite. I also thought you were kind…I could see it in your eyes. But I also saw distance there. You were wearing it as well as you wear your scrubs."

"You think I wear my scrubs well?" he teased.

"Now, that is definitely a speculation on your part." She laughed. "But if that is what I meant, I'm sure I'm not the first one to say it."

"But maybe you're the first one I've ever really heard saying it. Or wanted to hear say it. And that's *not* speculation."

Now, this was getting uncomfortable. Not making her feel awkward so much as ill at ease, as they'd gone from an impersonal chat to something that had the potential to become much too personal. She hadn't meant to start it, hadn't meant to make that comment about the way he looked in his scrubs, but it had just popped out. He was so easy to talk to, to sit next to on the floor and feel relaxed. Feel normal. Except she didn't get to be *normal*. Not any more. Consequently, that was going to make being anywhere near Rick a challenge. "Um… could we talk about the pediatric ward expansion for a minute?" she asked, not even caring that the transition was abrupt. All she knew was that she had to get out of *this* conversation, and get out fast! "I've been meaning to ask you how many square feet, overall, will be allotted for the entire department."

"Did I scare you, Summer?" he asked. "Because I didn't mean to."

The fact was, he didn't scare her. Quite the opposite, actually. And *that* was what scared her. "I have a lot on my mind, Rick. And a lot to do. I just don't want to get distracted. You can understand that, can't you?" Scooting away from him, she pushed her plate aside then stood up. "Alyssa and I have some adjustments to make now that I'm going to be working full time, and I just need to concentrate on what I have to deal with.

Right now, it's how to make my life work with the changes, and how to go about the changes that will make the pediatric department work. That's all." Sad, but true. Once upon a time, she'd been more dimensional. But that had been a long time ago.

"I've been there, Summer. When I set out on my life journey, I suppose you could call it, I was single, without too much going on except my medicine. Then one day I was a married man with a child on the way. I blinked my eyes, and I was a divorced, single father trying to figure out how to run a hospital and raise a child by myself at the same time. So I do understand how difficult it gets." He stood up and laid his plate next to the sink. "Now, how about I wash and you dry, since I don't know where anything goes?"

"Really? You want to help me with the dishes?"

He chuckled. "I don't know what kind of man you were married to before, but *real* men do dishes."

What kind of man had she been married to? The kind who would break a dish on the floor in a fit of anger rather than wash it. But Rick did dishes. In her book, that made him awfully close to being a keeper. Too bad she wasn't keeping.

It was a simple thing. For Mary Grace's coming-home dress, Edie wanted the little antique dress Grace's mother had put on Grace to bring her home from the hospital. Edie described it as yellowed by time, with lace. She'd found it at the beginning of her pregnancy, put it aside, and had apparently forgotten where it was as Summer couldn't find it where Edie thought she'd left it. Summer was looking everywhere. Not a simple task, going through drawers and closets, feeling more like a voyeur or sneak thief than a friend. She didn't like invading personal space, even if she had permission to do it. As someone who kept her own share of secrets, it didn't seem right looking through someone else's house, discovering things she wasn't meant to see, which was what this felt like. More than that, so many of Grace's effects were left behind. She was, quite literally, everywhere, which made Summer sad when she ran across them. So between tears that came and went when she stumbled onto something that reminded her of Grace, and nervousness, she knew she wasn't being as thorough as she should.

"Edie, I've looked through every single drawer in every bedroom," Summer said over the cellphone. "Are you sure Rafe didn't find it and put it somewhere you don't know about?"

"He might have, but he's tied up in surgery, and I can't ask him."

"Maybe we should wait." She loved Edie to pieces, but Edie was almost obsessed with finding this little dress. Of course, she did understand the sentiment because she, too, had loved Grace Corbett.

"Have you tried any of the closets yet? Maybe it's on a shelf somewhere."

"This house has a million closets, Edie, with a billion shelves. I've given them all a quick look but Grace had a thing for clothes, and they're all still here."

"So, try that big walk-in closet in her bedroom again. We cleared it out a little bit when we converted the room to the nursery, but I never got around to removing everything. It makes sense that I might have stuck that dress in the nursery closet, doesn't it?"

She sounded very hopeful, which was why Summer went back to the nursery for another look. This time, though, not in the drawers of a pink and white bureau painted with kittens and puppies but in Grace's cavern of a closet that, minus all the shelving, was large enough to be a room unto itself. Quite literally, it was larger than most bedrooms, with built-in shoe racks, motorized revolving clothes rails, a lighted dressing table, pull-out shelves, tucked-back shelves, a closet anteroom with pegs for belts and scarves. And Edie was right. She hadn't removed everything. It was still full of Grace, from shoes to hats, and even a couple of feather boas Summer was sure Grace must have worn to a costume party.

During thirty minutes of feeling around blindly at the backs of the various shelves, Summer accidentally knocked down a box of odds and ends. Old photographs, handwritten letters…family things she had no right riffling through. As she hurried to collect the spilt assortment and get everything back in the box, her cellphone rang. It was Edie again, telling her where, exactly, to find the dress. Apparently, Myra Murdock had come across it in a drawer, noticed a small tear, and taken it to do some mending and hand-laundering.

"It's wrapped in tissue paper on a shelf in the laundry room," Edie said.

"On my way to get it right now," Summer said, scooping the last of the papers into the box. As it turned out, the last one stopped her dead. It was an envelope, not yellowed like all the others but very white, very new in comparison. Addressed to Rick. *Rick Navarro. Important! Please read.* She recognized Grace's handwriting, felt an immediate chill up her spine.

The first thing that struck Summer was why it was virtually hidden, if Grace had thought this was so important. The second thing was, what to do? This really wasn't any of her business and she didn't particularly want to turn it into her business. But since Grace had meant Rick to see what was in the envelope… If nothing else, she was loyal to Grace. Which meant her sense of obligation was winning. So she dialed Edie.

"Did you know anything about a box of photos and old letters and papers Grace had put away in her closet? When I was looking for the dress, I knocked it down."

"I moved into Grace's house the way she left it, and I make new discoveries every day," Edie replied. "So, what's in the box that's got you calling me?"

"An envelope addressed to Rick marked 'Important', asking him to read it."

"He was one of the people under her wing," Edie said thoughtfully.

As so many had been. "Well, I thought somebody should know about it. I mean, it's none of my business, but I didn't feel right just putting it back in the box, then putting the box away. And it's really not my place to give it to Rick either."

"Bring the letter to the hospital when you bring the dress for Mary Grace and, in the meantime, I'll see if Rafe knows what it's about."

He didn't know. In fact, he had no idea about that box of photos. "I think Jess and I should go through it when we have time to sit down together," he said, handing the envelope addressed to Rick back to Summer. He arched playful eyebrows. "Maybe we'll discover something about Aunt Grace we never knew, like she had a secret lover, or she was a spy during the war. Anyway, would you give it to him for me? She wanted him to have it, so he should. I'm on my way back to surgery, or I'd do it myself." He kissed Edie, who was nursing Mary Grace, and kissed Mary Grace as well, then headed to the hall. Before he was totally out of the hospital room, though, he turned back to Summer. "You were closer to my aunt in her last months than anyone else. You wouldn't happen to know what's in the envelope, would you? Did she ever say anything to you?"

Summer shook her head. "Not a word. I know she really cared about Rick. Was very proud of him. But, no, I don't have any idea what's inside."

Rafe shrugged. "I suppose if Rick wants us to know, he'll tell us." He blew a kiss to Edie, then dashed off to surgery. Leaving Summer to dash off to Rick's office. Alyssa was with Mrs. Murdock and Molly for the afternoon, and Summer had promised to meet them at the city park in twenty minutes. It was a play date with her daughter for which she didn't want to be late, so she had to hurry.

"I have something for you," she said from

Rick's doorway. He was poring over patient charts, reading glasses on, hair mussed. All in all, an image that was going to stick with her for a while.

"Something good, I hope," he said, motioning her in.

"Actually, I don't know." She held out the envelope. "I found it in a closet at Gracie House a little while ago, and Rafe said I should give it to you. So..."

Pushing his reading glasses up first, Rick then took the envelope, studied the writing on the front, then looked at Summer. "From Grace?"

She nodded, then started to back away. "That's her handwriting."

"No, don't leave," he said, motioning her to the chair on the other side of the desk from him.

"But it's none of my business," she protested.

He grinned up at her. "And aren't you the least bit curious?"

"Well, maybe a little."

"Then sit. We'll do this together. I mean, what can it be?"

What, indeed? Even after her death Grace had proved to be a woman of many surprises. In other words, there was no telling what the envelope contained. Curiosity did get the best of Summer, though, and since Rick had asked her to stay, that was what she did. Only she stood behind him, to read over his shoulder.

And what they read together...

My dearest Rick,

If you're reading this, I'm gone and somebody's been cleaning out my effects. Just as well, because what I have to tell you is something I never could bring myself to say. But it's something you have a right to know.

First, please know that I've always cared about you. You were a smart boy, and it hurt me to know that Rafe and Jess bullied you. But they were young, their souls were tortured, and I hope that by the time you read this you will understand the kind of life they had with their father, because that life does affect you.

My brother, Lawrence, was a mean, disturbed man. I'll make no excuses for him, because he deserves no excuses. If there is a hell, that's where he is for what he did to his sons. But it's also where he is for what he did to your mother. Maria was a kind woman, very quiet, very dutiful. And very young when she came to work for my brother. To cut to the chase, your mother loved your father—Lawrence Corbett—and of that you were born. Did he love her in return? I don't know, but I doubt it, as Lawrence was a womanizer and I don't believe he was capable of loving anybody but himself. I can't even tell you why your mother stayed working for him for so many years, even when he was abusive to her, which I'm sure you know he was. Love does strange things to people, I suppose. All I can say is, your mother was an honorable woman who deserved better than what my brother gave her. Maybe the only answer lies in the way your mother cared for you. Perhaps she never knew she had other choices other than staying with Lawrence.

So you are my nephew, as much as Rafe and Jess are my nephews. And the three of you are brothers. Now, let me explain my complicity in this secret. At the end, when your mother was so sick and you were in medi-

cal school (please know that I endowed you
to medical school before I knew you were
my nephew, because you were deserving),
she sent for me to come to her, and she told
me everything. It broke her heart how you
were treated by the Corbett family. That's
why she'd always told you your father had
died before you were born. She didn't want
you experiencing the cruelty of an uncaring
family the way she had when she'd left her
family to come to America. They turned their
backs on her, disowned her. She understood
the pain of rejection, and wanted to protect
you from it.

When Maria knew she could not win her
battle against cancer, she didn't want you to
be alone in the world, and that's the reason
she revealed everything to me. She wanted
you to have me, and wanted me to have you.
But she didn't want you to know the truth, as
she feared you would hate her for the things
she'd done. Her greatest fear, however, was
that knowing the truth would hurt you. She
tried so hard to protect you, Rick. And,
yes, she made mistakes. But I think the only

*thing you can really say about your mother
is that while her intentions were good, she
was naive. Which was why, when she begged
me not to tell you the truth, I made the promise to her, and honored it. Yet I have always
felt guilty, as it's your right to know who
you are. You are a Corbett. You have family. And I have loved you every bit as much
as I have loved Rafe and Jess. Never doubt
your mother's love in trying to protect you
and, please, never doubt mine.*

"Oh, my…" Summer whispered when she'd read to the end. She looked down at Rick to see his reaction, and saw…well, nothing. He was simply sitting there, holding the letter in his right hand, balling his fist with his left. "Rick, I don't know what to say. Are you…OK?"

He shrugged. Sighed heavily. Didn't say a word.

"I think it's a good thing, what Grace did. It would have been as easy to—"

"To what?" Rick interrupted. His voice was a volcano on the verge of erupting, quiet at first but with the build-up of molten lava inevitable.

"Keep the secret of who I am to herself to protect me from who I really am? Or to protect Rafe and Jess from their bastard brother?" He dropped the letter on the desk, then shoved his chair back.

"So what are you going to do?" Summer asked, stepping around him to face him. "Go get all confrontational on them? The three of you are finally now getting along, so is it your plan to ruin that?"

"Plan? You mean I *get* to have a plan in my life? Because according to that letter, my mother and my aunt seemed to think their plans were more important than anything I could plan for myself."

He started to push himself out of his desk chair, but Summer intervened by pressing him back down before he could stand fully. "It's a shock. I get that. But what I also get is that you're not reacting the way you would if this was somebody else going through it."

"Then tell me, what am I supposed to do? Take a deep breath, count to ten, take another deep breath if I need it, keep counting to ten until I'm blue in the face?"

"Yes, if that's what it takes, because I can promise you that if you go storming out of here right now and confront either Rafe or Jess, you'll be doing something that will come back to haunt you, maybe even damage you for years to come. Or the rest of your life. And you've got Chris to think about, too. You're not in this alone any more. Those men are his uncles...*his blood relatives.* He has a right to know that, even if you don't want it. And whether or not you like it, Rafe and Jess have a right to know they have a nephew. So don't ruin this for Chris only because you're angry."

At the mention of his son's name, Rick did draw in that deep breath.

"Look, I know it's not easy, suddenly finding out you're not who you've always thought you were. But that's your bloodline, Rick. It's not you. Not the deep-down part of you that you've built into an amazing man."

"But I grew up in that man's house. My mother and I lived in...in literally the back room. She divided it so I could have my own private sleeping space while she slept on the couch. And he knew...Lawrence Corbett *knew* I was his son, and he didn't do better by us. In fact, in all the years I was there, he barely even spoke to me. And the way he treated my mother, the way he demanded she wait on him hand and foot..."

"He was a cruel man. When I worked for Grace, she told me about the things he did to Rafe and Jess. Rafe was beaten over and over, year after year. Jess was verbally abused, screamed at, belittled. In comparison, you were only ignored, not acknowledged as his son. I think that makes you the lucky one. That, and you had a mother who loved you very much. Rafe and Jess didn't have a parent who loved them, Rick. Think about that."

Shutting his eyes, Rick dropped his head back against his chair. "She should have left him."

Summer moved around behind Rick and gently, instinctively, she began to rub the knots out of his shoulders. He was tense, wound up, and the instant her fingertips started their easy kneading, he relaxed into her touch. "Why didn't she?" she asked. "Assuming that, over time, she quit loving him, why wouldn't she have left?"

"Because she was an illegal. At least, at that time she was. Eventually she got all her immigration papers and made everything right, but when my mother first came to the United States she didn't have a lot of options. She wanted a better life, didn't really think things through, and Lawrence Corbett was the one who looked the other way and gave her a job, as well as a place to stay." His shoulders tightened up. "And he took advantage of her situation. Saw a naive young girl and used her."

"Just relax," Summer said, understanding her words were merely platitudes. Rick's life had been turned upside down. Nothing that made sense to him only moments before made any sense now. She understood that. Understood it in huge, life-changing ways herself. Which was why she hadn't already left him alone to figure it out, or be angry about it, or punch his fist through the wall. She'd done all that, literally, figurative, in fantasy, and getting through it alone, and left to your own imploding devices, wasn't a good idea. She'd had Grace to help her, and Rick had…well, as far as Summer knew, he had no one. "Look, let's get out of here, OK? You need some time away from the hospital, time to think, to readjust. And I know a couple of horses that would love some exercise."

"And that will fix everything?" he quipped sarcastically.

"Nope, won't fix a thing. You've got some issues to deal with, some things you're going to have to make better in your head. But that's not going to happen this soon. It's going to be a process. So, as the person to whom you've entrusted your pediatrics ward, I'm giving you my medical opinion. You're really not fit to work right now. My prescription for that is a ride. Chris is with Mrs. Jenkins, I can call Myra and ask her to look after Alyssa for a little while longer. Then you've got no excuses, unless…" She stepped back in front of him. "Unless you don't want to be around me right now."

He looked up, gave her a half-chuckle. "I think maybe you're the only one I do want to be around right now."

She held out her hand to Rick. "Then let's go."

He took it, stood, but resisted her tugging him along toward the door. "There's something I need to ask you first. About what's in the letter…I'm not ready to talk to anybody about it yet. OK? Not even to my…my *brothers*."

"But you will at some point?"

Still holding onto Summer's hand, he shrugged. "If you hadn't found that box, if no one had ever found that box, we wouldn't be having this discussion, and my life would have gone on the way it has been."

She was quite aware that a simple tug toward the door had turned into holding hands, and she wasn't opposed to it. Wasn't ready to break the connection either because she liked the feel of his hand. Not smooth, as some would expect of a doctor. She could feel the calluses from hard work at the stables, and the roughness…a texture that made her tingle. "But I did find it, Rick. Everything *has* changed for you. And Rafe knows the letter exists. Not what's in it, but that you have it. So none of this is going to go away because you want it to."

"You're right. A ride will help me clear my head. How about we meet at the stables in half an hour? That'll give me time to run home and put on my riding boots."

And give her time to get over holding hands

with the chief of staff and brace herself to never, ever put herself in that position again. "Half an hour," she agreed, this time letting Rick tug her toward his office door. Once there, though, propriety took over, and they walked out separately, and separated, no one the wiser that she had goose-bumps running amok all over her arms.

CHAPTER FOUR

"IT's not the highest vista on Gracie Estate, but I used to like this place when I was a kid because no one else came here. When I was here I felt like I was alone in the world, that nobody could touch me here, or even get close to me, and I had a great sense of accomplishment connected to this place." He sighed deeply, fixing his focus on some unseen speck down below. "Rafe always went up to a bluff on the other side of the foot-hills. I didn't know it at the time, but I guess he and Jess would hide for days when Lawrence Corbett was on one of his rampages. And Jess had his own favorite place to go, somewhere closer to the lake, not so much for hiding as enjoyment. He's actually building a house there now for Julie and himself. But for me, this was where I always wanted to come when something, or someone, was bothering me because I had the best view of the sunrise and there was something about the sunrise and a new day that always made things seem better."

Rick dismounted his spirited stallion, a horse Molly Corbett had originally named Cupcake, and which Rick now called Patch, owing to a single black patch on an otherwise all-chestnut coat. "When I staked out my claim to this little corner of my world, I named it *Vista de Amanecer*, loosely translated to mean Sunrise Vista. Figured that with the way Rafe and Jess treated me, they owed me this much."

"It's beautiful. Stunning. And I'll bet the sunrises from here are spectacular." For a moment, an image of Rick watching the sunrise from here flashed through her head. She saw him as a strong boy, maybe a little bewildered, maybe a little hurt. But strong. Then she saw another image…one with her arm slipped though his, standing on the edge of the cliff with her head on his shoulder, and both of them gathering in the same breathtaking view. Even atop her horse, she could almost feel that strength in him. It ran through him like an underground spring… something always coursing below the surface yet not for public display. It was a quiet strength buried inside a serene man. More breathtaking than the view, actually. And these were unsafe thoughts. Dangerous daydreams. She wasn't entitled. So, literally shaking her head, trying to rid herself of the images fighting to take hold, Summer climbed down off Lacy, her white filly, also named by Molly, and followed Rick to the precipice, taking particular care not to stand too close to the edge, and especially not too close to him as she wasn't sure she could withstand the risk he posed her.

"I never had the chance to explore the estate very much after I moved here. Grace kept me pretty busy looking after her, volunteering at the foundation, just trying to keep up with her pace, and when I wasn't occupied doing something for her, or with her, I had Alyssa, who's a little on the young side to take too far. But since we live here now, and I don't intend going anywhere, I expect I'll have plenty of time in the future to look around. Maybe bring Alyssa out for a picnic someplace other than the kitchen floor. "

Rick chuckled. "It was original. Can't say that I've ever eaten a meal on the kitchen floor. I think your daughter has quite an imagination."

"And pretty strong powers of persuasion, as we actually *did* eat on a floor."

"Well, I don't know what your ex-husband was like, but I think Alyssa is a lot like you. Headstrong, smart, convincing. I know she's got Chris wrapped around her little finger."

"I think Chris is a lot like his dad. He may get wrapped around a little finger, but only as much as he wants to be. He'll know when it's time to unwrap and make the relationship more mutual."

"You're right. But it's too bad his dad didn't know how to unwrap himself the first time he got wrapped."

"Wrapped, as in marriage?"

Rick nodded. "As in marriage."

"But you got yourself unwrapped."

"More like she did it. Decided somewhere in her pregnancy that none of it was for her. Handed me the baby when he was born and said goodbye. Would have made life a lot simpler if I'd have unwrapped myself right after I met her, but, well…" He shrugged.

"Maybe so. But look what you got for your… shall we call it your little spot of trouble?"

"Little spot of trouble? That's choice!" He

laughed aloud over that one. "You sure do have a way of underplaying things. I've always thought my marriage and divorce were a huge blotch. But you know what? You're right. What I got for my little spot of trouble has rocked my world in ways I never thought it could be rocked."

And he was over the spot, blotch or whatever he wanted to call it. Completely over it. It wasn't following him the way her huge blotch was following her. That was a benefit he hadn't even been aware of.

"Too bad Grace thought she had to keep her secret," Rick continued, on a more nostalgic note. "Because Chris could have rocked her world, too. It would have been good for both of them. I mean, I don't know if it would have made things any different between Grace and me if I'd known she was my aunt, because we had a good relationship. But it would have been nice knowing that I had someone out there besides my mother, someone else with whom I shared a family bond. Maybe Chris could have benefitted from knowing he had an aunt. Maybe we all might have been a little closer."

"You mean the way she was close with Rafe and Jess?"

He shrugged. "Grace had different obligations with them. When I was young I didn't understand that, but I must have been eight or nine the first time I saw what they went through with their father...*my* father. Funny, but Rafe and Jess never refer to him as Dad or Father. He's always the old man. Guess I can't blame them for that, especially after what I saw...*the old man* was drunk, beating Rafe. We lived in the same house, but I never saw it, or pretended not to see it. I always suspected, but I didn't really care, maybe because I thought they deserved it for what they did to me. They kept it so...hidden, though. But this one time, I walked in on Rafe getting beaten. The old man bloodied his nose, broke his arm. Don't know what for, didn't stay around long enough to find out, it scared me so bad. Then I remember at school afterwards, Rafe talking about how one of the horses bucked him. Said he went over a corral fence, landed hard. He told everybody it was no big deal. But it was a big deal, because I knew the truth. And true to form, Rafe threatened to beat the hell out of me if I ever told.

"That's when the old man moved my mother and me out of the house and set us up in one of the cottages. Guess he wanted to hide what he was doing. Yet the truth of it kept coming back to me, over and over, year after year. I kept seeing the old man, seeing Rafe. Remembering all the times I saw bruises, black eyes… Remembering all the excuses Rafe and Jess made. And me, still thinking they deserved it. Yet there was my mother… I never saw bruises on her, but the way the old man yelled at her, and treated her like dirt…called her names no one should ever be called. He bullied her, Summer, and she let herself be bullied! *He means well, Ricardo,* she would tell me. *Nothing to worry about. He gives us a good home.* But I did worry, I *had* to worry, because no one else did. At least I didn't think they did, didn't know Grace did. And my mother just kept on working hard for that man, while all he ever did was…yell at her, belittle her." He cringed. "I don't even want to think of what else might have been going on, especially now that I know he was my father.

"The thing is, I always wondered why she stayed. It didn't make sense. *Anything* would have been better than the way she was treated. I mean, there were so many nights when she'd drag herself back from the main house, then lock herself in her bedroom and cry. I couldn't do anything to help her. Not a damned thing. And that's what bothered me most…*that she cried* and I couldn't comfort her." Rick turned away, to face a large boulder on the other side of the vista.

"I was angry at my mother for a long time, for letting herself be treated that way. Didn't speak to her, was pretty belligerent when I had to be anywhere near her. I even ran away once, when I was about fifteen or sixteen. Came up here and camped out for almost an entire summer so I didn't have to deal with her because she…she disappointed me. Summer, I *told* her she disappointed me, and the look on her face…if I live to be a hundred, I'll never forget it, never forget the pain I caused her. After I left, those were probably the worst few weeks of my younger life, dealing with my guilt over hurting my mother and trying to figure out why she stayed in an abusive situation with the old man."

Summer swallowed hard. "Did you ever figure it out?"

"Figure out what? That what my mother did happened all the time, that women stayed for any number of reasons? That my mother didn't care enough about herself to make it stop? Yet I loved her. So I steeled myself to the fact that she'd made her choices, went home and patched things up with her as best I could. But the relationship was never the same after that. She disappointed me, I hurt her. We got along, pretended nothing was going on. And I *never* said a word about any of it because my mother begged me not to. That's how we existed for years, and it took its toll. I lost things I'll never get back, and I didn't even know..." He paused, steadied himself with a deep breath. "He was my father."

"Would it have made a difference?" Summer asked.

"I don't know. Probably not to the old man. Nothing, or nobody made a difference to him. But it might have helped me understand my mother better. There was a time when she loved the man. It would have been nice knowing what she found to love. Nice for me, maybe even nice for Rafe and Jess, as they never saw anything but the cruelty in him."

"But your mother eventually did leave, didn't she?"

Turning back to face her, he nodded. "I'd gone to a college not too far from here, but when I was accepted into medical school it was half-way across the country and I refused to go if she didn't come with me. She desperately wanted it for me and taking her with me was the only way I could think of to keep her safe. I was so afraid that without me there, the old man might…" He choked off his words, drew in a ragged breath. "Anyway, Grace facilitated my mother's move by finding an apartment for her and a job where she was appreciated. Near my campus. It was a whole new life for both of us, and little by little I saw the life return to her eyes. And her smile… She didn't smile much when we were in Lilly Lake, but after she moved…she had such a beautiful smile. Anyway, I think those few years away from the old man were the only time I ever saw my mother happy. So, considering how Rafe and Jess had to grow up, they probably needed Grace and her special *ways* more than I ever would have. But I can't help feeling a little…"

"Cheated?" Summer asked.

Rick shook his head. "Sad's a better way to describe it, I think. Or disappointed."

"So, if Grace knew Rafe and Jess were being abused, and even your mother…"

"Why didn't she do something to stop it?" Rick's voice turned bitter. "In a word, clout. Lawrence Corbett was here first, his best friend was the local judge, he was the only doctor in town at the time. Take your pick. He kept this right and proper public facade and people accepted that. Trusted it or turned a blind eye to who he really was because his services were needed. Sometimes it's easier to turn a blind eye. It's what I did for so many years. In the end, he had a power Grace couldn't fight, because if she fought, and failed, Rafe and Jess would have been the losers. The old man wouldn't have let her anywhere near them."

"In other words, Grace saw herself as the one who had to be here to pick up the pieces afterwards, because there was nothing else she could do beforehand."

"Something like that."

"It must have been awful for her, watching what her brother was doing and not being able to stop him."

"Maybe fighting him the way she did by trying to undo his wrongs is what gave her strength. I just wish I'd known the truth. Even if that truth might have hurt me, it was my right to know it." His voice trailed off, then he regrouped. "Anyway, are you up to taking the trail over to my boulder?"

She glanced out at the boulder he'd pointed to moments before. "*Your* boulder? You have your very own vista as well as a boulder?"

"My name's on it so, as far as I'm concerned, that makes it mine." He straightened his shoulders and smiled with pride, the sense of achievement reflecting in his eyes. His vista, his journey—it was about entitlement and pride. In a young life those things were important. Surprisingly, they were important in an older life, too. "Inked my name there the first time I was brave enough to climb around and sit on it."

"I'm impressed. From what I'm seeing, that was a pretty amazing feat. It's scary up here. Nothing I'd be inclined to want to attempt, and I don't generally consider myself a wimp." Summer glanced at the trail, then she looked at the drop-off. It was wicked, with jagged rock face all the way down, complete with jutting shards until you hit the tops of the trees. If you were lucky enough to make it that far. And that was a great big *if*. The road to the bottom was a big, bad drop-off, and while she wasn't especially afraid of heights, this particular down slope was the very devil itself. Just looking down made her squirm. "Um…feel free to climb over there yourself if that's what you want to do, but I think I'll stay right here where I'm pretty sure both my feet will stay on terra firma." And wishing she had an anchor, or Rick, to hang onto.

He chuckled. "After I found this place, it took me nearly two years to gather up the courage to…shall we call it *walk the walk*? Time after time, I'd come up here full of plans to get over there…sometimes I'd stay awake at night thinking about it, planning how I was going to do it. Seeing it in my head, every step, every movement I'd have to make to ensure I wouldn't go plunging to my death. But I'd always change my mind next time I got here. Sometimes I'd try, get a few feet along the ledge, look down, maybe knock a chunk of rock off and watch it fall all the way to the bottom, then I'd climb my way back. Most of the time, though, I wouldn't even make it that far. I'd get to the edge and decide I was too smart to try something like that. But the challenge of it…that was *always* the thing for me. I wanted…*needed*…to get around to that damned boulder. It kept calling my name, reminding me that it was waiting for me."

"Since you left your indelible mark there, I know the end of the story. But what about the middle part where you actually went through with it? What was it that made you finally go all the way?"

One single, simple question and it was like a somber shroud dropped down over them. Ugly reminders of an ugly past he rarely talked about. Normally, his inclination would have been to change the subject, or fudge the details. But there was something about Summer that compelled him in other directions. She knew…

things. He wasn't sure what, but he saw it in her eyes. Something deep. Something desperate. Something she understood as well as he did. So he sucked in a deep breath, and began. "I'd barely turned thirteen, felt all grown up being a teenager. It was my birthday, my mother had made a cake for me and invited in a few of my school friends to help me celebrate…not Rafe and Jess, by the way. But they came anyway. Barged right in. Rafe shoved me around in front of my friends, Jess made fun of my homemade cake, knocked it off the table. We got into a fight… Rafe and I bloodied each other up pretty badly. Jess jumped into the middle of that one, and I didn't stand a chance against the two of them. It turned into a horrible day. I was humiliated, and all I wanted was to go somewhere nobody could find me, and never come back. So I came up here, brooded for a while. Don't know what came over me other than the need to prove myself, or to do something they couldn't, so I squeezed myself all the way around that ledge and staked my claim on that boulder. Anyway, I liked it there. Felt like the king of the world. Then I spent a lot of time there over the years when I needed to get away or just to think. I felt invincible, like when I was there, nothing could touch me."

"And now? Do you still come up here when you need to get away, or think?"

"Haven't been back out on the boulder for a while. Several years, actually. No time, no point. Maybe that youthful naivety that I'm invincible has faded. Or my problems don't seem bigger than the world. Whatever the case, it's still nice to come up here to the vista to clear my head every now and then." He smiled a devilish little grin. "And still know that neither Rafe nor Jess has ever been to the boulder."

Summer laughed. "So there's still some rivalry left after all?"

"Not really. When I got my *adult* thinking on, I understood why they did what they did. Understood it and even felt bad for them. I mean, it was all a reaction to what the old man was doing. Their way of striking back where they could. Sure, that doesn't diminish the way I felt when I was a kid and they were bullying me, and I'd be lying if I told you those feelings don't rear their ugly head from time to time, because they do. The hurt that some children experience never goes away. It's true of me, the way it's also true of Rafe and Jess. But I'm in control of my emotions now, or I like to think I am, and I can deal with them without having to react. Besides, both Rafe and Jess have apologized. So now this place is only about the view for me." He pulled her over to a couple smaller rocks, where they sat down. "I've never seen a better one. And when Chris is a little older, I'll bring him up here with me."

"What if he wants to climb around to your boulder?"

Rick cringed. "I think the most difficult part of parenting is trying to protect your child in general and, specifically, trying to protect them from all the mistakes you made."

"But was climbing around to the boulder a mistake? Or was it something very necessary in the life of a young boy?"

"OK, let me amend what I just said. I think the most difficult part of parenting is trying to protect your child in general and, specifically, trying to protect them from all the mistakes you made, while at the same time helping to balance their need for independence as well as recognizing that experience is the best teacher." He chuckled. "And that last part might have to include locking them in their room until they're an adult."

"So what you're telling me is that as Chris is six, you'll protect him. But in seven years, when he wants to climb around to the boulder, you'll respect his need for independence?"

He chuckled. "Maybe it's easier to never tell him this place exists."

"But he'll find his own boulder, Rick."

"And I'll have to do one hell of a parenting job until then to make sure he knows how to tackle that boulder when the time comes."

"Because you're a good father." The kind of father she wished Alyssa had. Truth was, her daughter's father was more like Lawrence Corbett than she cared to think about. And it was interesting, hearing Rick's reaction to his father…but hearing it from the perspective a child had. The perspective Alyssa might have had if they'd stayed with Cameron any longer. Without knowing it, Rick had confirmed that she had been right to leave. More than that, he'd made her realize that what Alyssa might have seen could stay with her, impact her in hurtful ways. She'd never really given that any consideration because she'd been so overwhelmed by her own abuse. But now that she knew, she would be prepared to deal with it. Her heart went out to Rick for his pain, but his pain had become part of her cure. For that, she leaned over and kissed him on the cheek.

"What was that for?" he asked, quite surprised.

"For the beautiful vista." And the lesson.

"Well, shoot. I wish I had another vista to give you."

"Don't get carried away. One vista is all I need, and one kiss is all you get…" One safe place, with someone she trusted. "And I like this one because you can see my house down there." She pointed off in the distance, to the white cottage she'd grown so attached to in such a short time. "Grace was very generous, giving that to me. I knew why I was coming here when I accepted her offer, but I had no idea that I would be staying here afterwards, that she would be the person who finally gave me my roots. And roots for Alyssa as well."

"You didn't have that before?"

Summer shook her head. "Not really. I did the bad marriage thing, too. Nothing worth talking about, really." She sincerely hoped Rick would take the hint, because after hearing what he'd said about his mother, hearing all his bitter feelings about why she'd stayed when she was being abused, Summer was afraid his feelings for her would be much the same if he knew her circumstances. How could Rick's mother have stayed with Lawrence Corbett? *How could she have stayed with Cameron?* Truth was, she didn't have an answer. Like Rick's mother, she, too, had made her choices. But, thank God, only for a little while. Because unlike Rick's mother, who had been a struggling immigrant, *she* had had the freedom to run.

"Then we won't, because that would ruin the feeling up here."

"It's a nice feeling, too," she said, glad to get off the gloomy subject and concentrate on the view. "And just think, Rick. It's all yours, too. At least, a third of it is."

He twisted to face her. "What do you mean by that?" he snapped.

Summer was caught off guard by his reaction as Rick was always so even-tempered, so pleasant all the time. Didn't he know? As close as he was to the family, even with his little bit of distance, she'd assumed he did know the conditions of the will. "I'm sorry. I though you were aware that Grace left her estate divided equally between her nephews. Not between Rafe and Jess, but her *nephews*. You're her nephew, Rick. That means you have a legal claim here."

He thought about it for a moment, stood up, paced over to the edge of the vista, stood there quietly, trying to let Summer's words sink in then, finally, turned around to face her. "She probably wrote the will before she knew I was included in that little group."

"No, not really. She drew up a new will about two months before she died. I was the witness. She specifically said *nephews*. Her lawyer questioned that, in fact. He told her she should mention Rafe and Jess by name, but she refused. I really didn't think much about it at the time, because Grace was a stubborn woman who had her own ideas about things. But it makes sense now. She knew by then you were her nephew, but she was still keeping her promise to your mother by not telling. Then, when the truth came out, you were covered."

"Why not include her letter with the will, then? If she wanted me included in the inheritance, why not admit it rather than hiding that letter away, like she did?"

Well, so much for the nice feeling. "Maybe she intended to. After all, Grace never really thought she was going to die. In fact, she'd taken on chairing a new committee only the day before she… Anyway, it could be something as simple as she thought she had more time to get everything done. Could be she wanted to tell Rafe and Jess first so they'd be prepared…and they weren't exactly coming back to Gracie House at that time. Or maybe she felt guilty not telling you, and she was simply trying to figure out how to do it, so she wrote the letter, had second thoughts and put it away until she decided how best to approach you. I guess we'll never know why she did it the way she did, but the one thing I do know is that she never meant to be cruel or unfair to you. If she had, she wouldn't have written the letter."

"And hid it."

"Was it hidden, or was it just tucked away for safekeeping until she was ready to tell everybody the truth? Maybe she'd screw up the courage, then lose it. You know, wrote the letter then had second thoughts. I mean, think about it, Rick. That one simple letter will change a lot of lives. Jess was isolating himself in that cabin out by the lake when he did come home, Rafe wouldn't come home at all. Hadn't come home in thirteen years. And Grace was dying. Could be some of it slipped her mind. Or she did have a plan that didn't come to pass."

"Doesn't matter. None of this has ever been mine anyway, and I've never been part of the family who owned it, even when I lived in their house. My father didn't acknowledge me, my mother spent a lifetime lying to me, and my aunt honored a promise she should have never made. So what, in that scenario, would make anybody think I'd want a piece of all this, when the only thing it represents is how shoved aside I was?" He shook his head. "Rafe and Jess can keep it, every square inch of it."

"What about the hospital? That's yours, too."

"Damn," he muttered. "That complicates things, doesn't it?"

"Not if you don't want it to. If you don't plan on telling them what you know, nothing will change and no one will be the wiser."

"But as part owner, I have a different level of responsibility. Being chief of staff was enough. Probably more than I ever expected. Being a co-owner, though..." He shut his eyes, drew in a deep breath... "I haven't mentioned this to anybody, but a couple weeks ago Rafe and Jess asked me to go in with them as a co-owner. They were simply going to give me one third of the hospital's ownership. Told me I deserved it since I was the one who'd taken care of the hospital these past few years." Opening his eyes, he stared, point blank, at Summer. "I turned them down. Didn't even think about it. Told them I had enough responsibility already, that I was happy with things the way they were."

"Why?"

He shrugged. "Maybe some of that childhood resentment's still left in me. Maybe I felt like they were offering me some kind of contrition compensation. You know, a pity gesture. I honestly don't know why I turned them down, but I did."

"How did that end?"

"They were both surprised, but they left the offer open. Told me if I changed my mind, to let them know and they'd see to the paperwork."

"I don't really know Rafe or Jess very well, but do you think they already suspected you're their brother? Could they have been trying to get on your good side by making an offer like that before you discovered you already were a co-owner?"

He didn't even think about that scenario before he rejected it with the shake of his head. "No, that's not it. In spite of our bad history, they wouldn't be that manipulative, especially with the hospital at stake. In fact, they've been generous, almost to a fault, endowing all the programs I've wanted to implement...endowing them from their own pockets rather than having the hospital dip into its operational funds. All that expansion going on right now is happening because Rafe and Jess do care, which has been a huge change of heart since neither one of them wanted to keep the hospital after Grace died.

In fact, they were looking to sell it. So their intentions are above board, and I don't have any reason to question them. And to be honest, if circumstances were different, I could probably be good friends with both of them."

"But circumstances *are* different."

"Which is the problem. Rafe and Jess probably have a right to know we shared a father, but I don't feel any particular urge to tell them. At least, not right now. And before you say something again about Chris's right to know, I get it. Maybe he does. I haven't figured out that part of it yet."

"Well, I'm not going to pressure you, Rick." She had no right to. Not with the kind of pressure she'd gone through for a good part of her adult life. Besides, they were friends…friends who now shared a pretty big secret. That made her a trusted part of his life, and she took that seriously. "If you want to talk about it, or use me as a sounding board, feel free as I'm the only one who knows what was in that letter. But so you'll know, in my own life I don't want anybody pressuring me about anything, so I'd never do that to anybody else." She glanced at her watch. "And in the meantime, I really do need to get back to Alyssa. Myra's being a saint, watching her, but I miss her." She stood up. "Oh, and I'll be fine going back by myself. I think you need a little more thinking time up here. So…I'll see you tomorrow, at the hospital."

"Are you sure?" he asked, walking over to her.

"Trust me, Rick. If there's one thing I'm very good at, it's taking care of myself."

"Can I at least walk you to your horse?"

What a quaint, old-fashioned gesture. And such an honest one, yet it made her feel…special. "I'd love to have you walk me to my horse."

So they strolled the short distance quietly. Not linking arms, not holding hands, which she wouldn't allow. Merely walking alongside each other, which she would. Then once they'd come to Lacy, Rick did the gentlemanly thing, making sure the stirrups were tight, the saddle was squared. He was about to offer Summer a leg up, but she deferred that particular gesture with the wave of her hand and pulled herself into the saddle with all the skill and grace of the accomplished horsewoman she was. "Thanks for bringing me up here," she said, looking down at him. "I like it so much I may have to find my own special place on the estate."

"Or share mine," he suggested. "And, Summer, thanks."

"For what?"

"For listening. For telling me the truth. Giving me advice. Caring. Putting up with my contentious ways."

"You're not so contentious. Maybe hardheaded, but I wouldn't call that contentious. Anyway…I'll see you tomorrow, Rick," she said, turning her horse and heading off down the trail.

In the distance, a small, private plane was buzzing well above the trees. Its drone was what she focused on as she descended the trail. Otherwise she would have been thinking about Rick.

CHAPTER FIVE

"It looks simple enough," Summer said absently, referring to the hospital's new computer system as she settled down to her brand-new desk. She had an office now, as well as a makeshift day-care center, which was situated in half the space it would eventually occupy. One small change, just the addition of the day care, with hand-picked staff, and Summer was relieved, knowing Alyssa was only just down the hall, safe with Anita Johnson. No, it wasn't the best plan. Being with Alyssa *all the time* was what she really wanted. But nursing was such a huge part of her, and she did want some of that life back. Otherwise Cameron won again. Then there was Alyssa, who was striking out, trying to find her independence in her own world. Here, her daughter's independence was fostered yet protected. So, even though this first day where her separation anxiety was its highest, overall this was good.

"It *is* simple, but I'll bet your mind isn't on the program we were discussing, is it?" Rick said, jolting Summer back to the present.

"It is. Well, maybe not totally."

"I looked in on Alyssa on my way down here, and she's fine. Has two other little friends in there with her, and Anita has everything under control."

"Thank you, Rick. I appreciate it. I keep wanting to go down there just to take a peek, but I'm rationing myself to once in the morning, at lunchtime, and once in the afternoon. So far, so good."

"We do have security cameras in there, like we do everywhere else in the hospital. So if it gets worse, you can go down to the security office and take a look at one of the monitors."

"Then I'd feel like I'm spying on her."

He grinned. "Which you would be. But Alyssa will never know."

"I'll know, though. And that's the point. She may only be four, but she does need her own life, too. Logically, I know that. Emotionally, though, it's not so easy to deal with."

"But in your heart you're a very good mother, who wants to take care of her child. You'll survive this, Summer. Each day it will get easier."

"Promise?"

He nodded. "Promise. And in the meantime, nail biting is allowed. I felt the same when Chris was four, and I decided he needed a couple hours a day in a pre-school situation, something to give him better social skills. Made me nervous as hell, even though Mrs. Jenkins already looked after him a good bit of the time. But I was used to Mrs. Jenkins, trusted her implicitly. This was pre-school. Chris was fine, took to it like a little trouper, and it got better when I realized that Chris was really thriving in his environment."

"Well, I like my nails," she said, holding up her perfectly manicured set. "So maybe I *will* have to become acquainted with the security office. That doesn't mean I'll be running down there every few minutes, but if I do catch myself with the urge to bite, I'll know it's there."

"Good for you."

Good for me, she thought to herself. And damn

Cameron to hell for turning her into what she'd become. "Wouldn't it be nice if parenting came with one comprehensive guidebook that had a single, definitive answer for every situation any parent might find themselves in?" She glanced up at him. Saw the blush creep to his cheeks. "What? You've bought parenting books?

"Maybe one or two. But only when I've run out of answers."

"Find any answers? Or, shall I say, any *good* answers?"

"What I found is that parenting is the hardest thing I'll ever do in my life. Other than that, it's a large part trial and error and, to some extent, growing up along with your kid. Raising Chris alone, one thing I've learned more than anything else is just how un-grown-up I was before he came along. He teaches me something new every day. Something that forces me to grow up a little more. And if I am totally honest about it, I'd say it's something that forces me to grow up a little more every time I make a mistake."

"And here we were, thinking the growing process was over with a long time ago. Anyway, thank you for hiring Anita. She's a gem, and once I get over my jitters, you'll have my undivided attention."

"Does that mean that I can have your *divided* attention right now?"

"Every last speck of it. Because you're a nice man, Rick. A good boss, but a very nice man."

"Ouch! Normally, being called *nice* is the kiss of death in a relationship. You know, *you're nice, but...* Then it follows up with something like *I'm moving to the Antarctic for the next decade but I'll call you up when I come back.* Or *I'd love for you to be in my wedding party.*"

Summer laughed. "Sounds like the voice of experience."

"I've been called nice a time or two."

"And..."

He shrugged. "I actually take it as a compliment...to a point. If we were involved, say, other than we are...you know, romantically, this is where my shoulders would slump and I'd turn away and slink out the door feeling dejected. But since we're not, this is where I'm going to grab hold of your divided attention and say...the computer program, which is what I'm really here to talk about, is easy to use. We had it designed specifically for our services here because it will keep everybody logged into the vital hospital functions, pretty much on the same page..." He glanced over at Summer, and she was laughing. "What?"

"Did you really come down here to talk computer programs, or were you checking to make sure I wasn't popping tranquilizers by the bucketful?"

"What if I said computer?" he asked, grinning sheepishly.

"Then I'd say you're not a very good liar, and I'd tell you what I tell Alyssa when she fibs, that I can see it in her eyes. But if you really do want to redeem yourself and make this about a computer program..."

"Do you really see it in my eyes? I know I can see it in Chris's eyes. Actually, his mouth twitches, too."

"And instead of being a disciplinarian, let me guess. You have to conceal a laugh because when he lies, then twitches, he's so cute you can't help yourself."

"It is cute...in Chris."

She smiled. "Not bad in his father either, that

little twitch you get sometimes. Also, it's a good thing to be aware of when you're dealing with your boss. Could come in handy someday."

"I twitch?"

Standing right there before her, Rick blushed. The second time she'd seen it happen. He turned a deep crimson, which stained beautifully against his bronzed skin, and might have gone unnoticed by most because it was subtle. But she noticed—like she noticed so many of the little things about Rick—his gentle hands, his kind smile, his melodious laugh. And while she really shouldn't be looking at him like that, she couldn't help herself because she liked all of what she saw, including his blush. "Just a little."

"And do you conceal a laugh because it's so cute?"

This chat was too cozy, too intimate. She had to get herself out of it fast before she started twitching, only in her it would be nerves. "Actually, I stare you straight in the eye and say let's take a walk around the area I have in mind for improvements to the pediatric ward, so I can tell you some of the things I've come up with. I've spent a good bit of time these past few days working on some ideas I've had, and I'd like your impression." Anything to get her away from this moment, the moment when she knew, for certain, her feelings for Rick were deepening.

"Um, sure. Why not?"

"I'm really excited about this, Rick. Hospitals are such scary places for children, and my ideas…I think they can turn a dreary hospital ward into a place where children aren't afraid to come." Strolling through the hospital hall, keeping a respectful distance apart, Rick and Summer stopped outside the family waiting room. "Like this place. I can see it as a solarium." Summer looked up, gazed for a moment at the ceiling. "No more white-tile ceilings. Glass. Sun during the day. At night, the stars. I think it will make the visitors feel better…I mean, the stress of having to be here because your child is sick is overwhelming. Sitting around, waiting for news. Scared. At least, I'd be scared if Alyssa was sick and I was the parent who had to be here. So I want to make this area special for them, a calm place where walls and ceilings won't close in around them. More than that, though, it would be a lovely place to bring the children...the ones who aren't able to go outside to my fairy garden—I'll tell you about that another time—or the ones who are too old for it. Maybe we can have a nook with video games and computers, a place where they can do what kids do but not in the confines of their hospital rooms."

He wasn't sure what he liked more—her idea, or watching her present her idea. She was animated, her eyes sparkling. Beautiful. *Extraordinarily* beautiful. But that beauty was enhanced by her passion for nursing. It had taken a while to convince Summer to accept the position, but she was well worth the wait. And just listening to her talk about her vision tangled him up in an enthusiasm he hadn't felt before. Turning a basic waiting area and a couple of superfluous offices into a solarium? Besides being a brilliant idea, it was necessary. She'd twisted him into a believer in a few simple words, and it was like he was seeing this dreary area through *her* eyes, because he caught Summer's vision, understood it. Taking care of the spirit, healing the body. It was all part of the same mission. To

Summer, though, it wasn't just about dispensing pills, taking X-rays, administering therapy. It was about letting the sun in, and Summer was that sun. "Well, I can't speak for the architects, because the renovation could be a real structural challenge, but I think it's worth exploring the possibility."

"Can we also, then, explore the possibility of a separate cafeteria for the pediatric area...for the parents and families of children in the ward? The main cafeteria is fine, but it caters more for adult food, things I might eat that Alyssa will not. I'd like to make the whole pediatrics department family friendly, and I think food oriented toward that end could be a great start. You know, serve healthy meals but meals that the siblings of our patients will enjoy, as in take care of the whole family while we're treating one member. Oh, and in the vending-machine area, get rid of the soft drinks and candy bars and try fruit juices and healthy snacks, maybe vend fresh fruit, yogurt."

Rick chuckled. "Something tells me there's more where that came from."

"Well, I do have some redecorating ideas for

the patient rooms. Less institutional, more like a children's hotel. Oh, and pets… I know we can't have a general policy allowing pets to visit, but I think we can set aside an area where parents can bring a family pet on a scheduled basis. Animals go a long way in a healing process, and since some of our children have extended stays, can you think of anything that will make them happier than visits from Fluffy or Fido? And along that line, therapy dogs on a regular basis. And in the solarium a large aquarium…"

"Whoa…slow down," Rick said, thrusting out both hands to stop her. "I can't keep up."

"Sorry," she said, laughing. "You can probably tell that I'm excited by the potential here. We can make a difference in pediatrics, Rick. Not just be another hospital that offers pediatric services, but be the hospital that makes a difference in the lives of sick children. Even small changes will help. Like this…" She pointed to the nursing station. "I'd like one central nursing station as a hub, with smaller stations positioned in the different hallways. It will save steps for the nurses, keep them closer to their patients by having the smaller stations spread out, and make the main station more efficient in that there won't be so many people hanging around it all the time."

Ambling on, they passed the nurses' station, a utilitarian little stop that offered nothing but the basics…medicine storage, computer, work area. Summer was right. Improvements here could make a huge difference in efficiency. Amazingly he'd passed this station hundreds of times and never even thought about it. Summer had a keen eye for the detail. Something he was admiring more and more each passing moment.

"And we need new lights. Something more natural. All this fluorescence is draining. And ergonomic desks and chairs would be good, too. Oh, and I think we could add a couple of class-rooms, and have tutors come in so the children won't miss their schooling. Also grandmothers… we need volunteer grandmothers to read stories. And rocking chairs in the rooms for the younger children, so parents can sit and rock them."

"Of course, we need rocking chairs and grand-mothers!" She was just brimming with enthu-siasm, something he was finding quite…sexy. Sexy to the point he was having a terrible time concentrating on anything but Summer. *His* bout with divided attention. Too bad his life couldn't be different, couldn't accommodate more, like an honest-to-God relationship with, well…her. But experience held him back. The first time in what he'd thought was a *real* relationship and he'd been burned, which didn't matter as it hadn't affected anybody but him. He'd walked away hurt but wiser. With that, he'd also walked away holding his son in his arms, promising himself that he'd be smarter in the future. That he wouldn't look and leap almost simultaneously, the way he had with Lana. But then the trust thing came up again, only with people he loved. His mother, Grace… Too much! More experience that had taught him he was just fine on his own. If there was no one around to trust, there was no one around to ill-use that trust.

Only thing was, one look at Summer…*his very first look*…and he'd wanted to leap. Wanted it bad. Which was why he had to keep his emotional distance right now. Besides, Summer was distant in her own right, and struggling with her own trust issues. She'd leapt badly once herself. He didn't know how bad, but it had isolated her, which meant the breach had to be devastating for her. So, no, he wouldn't think about Summer in anything other than a casual way.

Yet his very first look...

"And I'm on board to support everything you've come up with, but I don't want you getting disappointed if Rafe and Jess are a little more conservative in what they want to do."

"But you support all of it?" she asked, smiling.

"All of it." It was like she hadn't expected anything from him, and he didn't know whether to be disappointed by that or not pay any attention to it. What was her impression of him, anyway? Maybe that's the thing he should have been thinking about most. Lana had thought him dispensable which, to her, he had been. And Summer...did she think him not supportive? Admittedly, that did let him down a bit because he'd thought, well...actually, it didn't matter what he thought. Summer was merely reflecting what he'd already decided on, that this relationship wasn't going to happen. "The thing is, the medical necessities come first. An aquarium is nice, but I've got to see to the medical priorities before we tackle the non-medical."

"So when you say medical, you mean like ded-

icated pediatric surgery? And pediatric intensive care?"

He raised surprised eyebrows, amazed how
she'd taken his one drawback and converted it
into her positive. "You'd turn this into a stand-
alone pediatric hospital if you could, wouldn't
you?"

Summer smiled. "If I could."

"Well, I think the next step will be taking these
ideas to Rafe and Jess to see what they think.
What you've come up lays out an entirely different picture than anything I've thought about.
Or anything Rafe and Jess have considered, for
that matter. Don't know if they'll be agreeable
to everything, but…" he shrugged "…we'll see."

"What happens if, when you hire a medical
director for the unit, he or she doesn't like my
ideas? What if…?" She paused, blushed, tilted
her head to look down. "That sounds conceited,
doesn't it?"

A gentle wisp of hair fell across her face and
he was very tempted to reach over, brush it back.
Wanted to feel the softness of her cheek against
his hand. Linger there for a moment, to enjoy…
In fact, the urge was overtaking him so hard he

had to physically restrain himself from reaching over to her then force himself to step out of an arm's reach. He cleared his throat. "Not conceited. Just..."

Suddenly the red light over the door down the corridor commenced flashing, while at the exact same time an automatic page over the public address system summoned staff to an emergency. "Dr Langly, Dr Navarro, Room 118. Stat. Dr Langly, Dr Navarro..."

Hearing the page, Rick ran directly to the room, while Summer spun around to the nurses' station, grabbed the crash cart and followed him. "Is she arresting?" he called out to the nurse, Corinne Amos, on his way through the door, then immediately spotted that the child was indeed seizing. "History of seizure disorder? Any other seizures on record?" he asked, pulling out his stethoscope to have a listen to the girl's chest. Heather Anderson's tiny body was jerking wildly on the bed, and she was bathed in sweat...sweat that had already soaked through the bed sheets.

"No seizures, according to her parents," Summer supplied on her way through the door. "No cardiac problems, no respiratory ailments.

Basically, she's a healthy eight-year-old who's had flu for over two weeks and can't shake it. They took her to their family doctor in Mosley, who said it was nothing. Brought her here to have her admitted yesterday late afternoon. So far, her admission has been uneventful. Until…"

Rick, nodded, impressed with Summer's thoroughness and her knowledge of her patient. Then laid his hand across the child's forehead. "Her temperature?" he asked, looking at Corinne.

"Just barely over one hundred, when I took it last time I was in here, twenty minutes ago."

"Then she's spiked in the last twenty minutes," he said, stepping back as Summer shoved to the forefront to take the child's temperature.

"A hundred four and a half," she said, in a matter of seconds.

"Febrile seizure," Rick diagnosed, as another floor doctor ran into the room. "But she's convulsing too hard, which tells me there may be something else going on, so I'd like to control this one." Often, in cases of convulsions resulting from high temperatures, the normal course was to let the child ride it out if the duration was short-lived. But for Heather, her seizure activity was bordering on violent, and Rick didn't want the child to hurt herself or have a brain bleed or stroke.

"Benzodiazepine?" Summer asked, already poised to inject it into Heather's IV.

Rick gave her the nod as Corinne struggled to take Heather's blood pressure and Dr Jane Langly got on the phone to call the child's parents in order to re-check her medical history, specifically to determine if they'd left out any pertinent facts.

"I need a cooling blanket," Summer called to another of the floor nurses who'd come in to help.

"And bring me something to test her blood sugar," Rick shouted after her. Too often, these kinds of things resulted from elevated blood glucose, something that could easily get out of whack during a prolonged illness like flu.

After the medicine was injected, Summer slipped an oxygen mask over the child's face. "I'll get an EKG, EEG and a head CT ordered stat…" She glanced over at Rick. "If that's want you want to do, Doctor."

He returned a barely perceptible smile. "That's

exactly what I want to do, Nurse." Then bent back over Heather to have another listen to her chest. In a matter of seconds she was already responding to the medicine, her small body still thrashing but not as wildly. Her eyes started to become responsive.

"Her parents claim she has no medical condition," Jane Langly called out. "But the mother did admit that Heather has had small convulsions prior to this, but only when she's sick."

"And she didn't think to tell us?" Rick snapped. "OK, well, I think we'll go on an expedition with this young lady to see if we can figure out why she's not shaking the flu like she should, and why she's prone to these small convulsions. After we get through the tests for this episode, I'd like an MRI and a full blood panel including electrolytes and an arterial blood gas."

He looked down at Heather, and smiled as she finally opened her eyes. "Welcome back, young lady. You've had us pretty worried."

Heather didn't say a thing at first, but large tears formed in her eyes, then spilled down her cheeks. "I think I had an accident," she said timidly.

Summer took hold of the girl's hand. "As soon as we shoo all these people out of here, we'll get you all cleaned up, put some fresh sheets on your bed…" She bent down and whispered, "And I have a princess tiara that will make you look beautiful."

"A princess tiara?" Rick questioned.

"Even when a girl isn't feeling her best, she still wants to look her best, *Doctor*." She gave him a saucy wink. "Sometimes it's just as important as the medicine we dispense."

"Oh," Rick said, clearly not understanding, but not willing to argue the point. "Then…" he shrugged "…I suppose we should leave you to it, shouldn't we?"

Summer nodded, as one of the nurses handed her a glucose test kit. "So, everybody…" She gave them the get-out-of-here wave of her hands, then prepared Heather for the finger stick.

Two hours later, Heather was clean, looking gorgeous in her princess tiara, and finished with all the tests Rick had ordered. Her temperature was down, not normal but much better, thanks to a cooling blanket, she'd been given her first of a lifetime of doses of insulin to control her

childhood diabetes, and she was sleeping peacefully, totally exhausted from her ordeal. As her
parents sat next to the bed, looking worried as
well as embarrassed for their deliberate act of
omission, Summer took one last check of the
girl's vital signs, then slipped out there door and
ran, quite literally, into Rick, who was standing
there, waiting.

"This isn't a one-time incident with elevated
blood sugar," he said.

"Like you suspected."

"Well, that was one of several things it could
be. But I just got the results of her blood sugar
readings taken over a course of weeks, and it
was well over the norm. I'm betting this has
been going on for a while. Over-indulgent parents who don't want to see, or admit, the problems happening. A child whose blood sugar
levels are probably bouncing up and down all
the time. An admitting doctor at the hospital in
Mosley who doesn't look beyond the obvious.
All of it gets you a child who's been pretty sick
for quite a while."

"Well, at least we know now. The untreated
diabetes explains her prolonged illness, which

explains the spiked fever. Poor thing. I'll bet she's been feeling miserable, even when she wasn't sick."

"Poor thing" was right. It made him stop and wonder what kind of mother Lana would have been to Chris. She'd known before she was three months into her pregnancy that she didn't want to be a mother, and had given up her baby almost at the moment of having him. In her favor, she'd done what she'd thought was best for her son. Now, in the next few days, Heather's parents were going to have to take a crash course in what was best for their daughter...something other than looking the other way. "You were good in there, Summer. We really haven't had much occasion to work together, but I'm...impressed. It's almost like you were reading my mind."

"Not reading your mind. Just anticipating that you're going to make the right calls." She smiled. "And you hired me to be good."

"But there's good, then there's *good*. I like the way you stepped up."

"And almost overstepped?" she questioned.

He shook his head. "No ego here. It's about the patient, and I'm glad to have someone working with our patients who's willing to take the lead. It will save lives. Ever thought about becoming a doctor?"

Summer laughed. "Nope. I'm doing what I'm supposed to be doing. Love everything about it. Wouldn't want to change."

"It's a good feeling, knowing you're doing what you're supposed to do. So, can I buy you a cup of coffee before we call it a day?"

She shook her head. "But, on the way home from work, if I could persuade you to buy me an ice cream with sprinkles…"

"Blue ice cream?"

"Blue's not so bad. But this time I feel like something…pink."

"Pink, like the tiara you put on Heather? Could you tell me what that was about?" he asked, as he turned, and gestured for Summer to follow him down the hall.

"It's simple, really. After a child has had a major crisis, it's very easy, and quite natural for them to dwell on it, to stay scared. Any of us would, I think. So I like to distract them with something normal. For a little girl like Heather, it's looking pretty. Another child might like a book, another to fix something, put it back to-gether, restore it. When you get the children caught up in something other what just hap-pened to them, they adjust to it better, and get over it much more quickly. Same with kids with prolonged illnesses. Like Amy Cavanaugh. She loves dressing up every day, even when she's going to chemotherapy. Ties a pretty scarf on her head, puts on sparkly shoes…it keeps her spirits up, even though she's so sick."

"Amazing," Rick commented.

"In a way, it is. Magicians do it by refocusing their audience's attention and—"

"Not the result. The nurse. She's what's amaz-ing. So, pink ice cream. That could be straw-berry, cherry, peppermint…"

"With sprinkles," she reminded him.

"Extra sprinkles."

Extra sprinkles, no children tagging along. This could almost turn into a date. Almost…

CHAPTER SIX

"NOTHING'S going on," Rick said. "Not a damned thing." He didn't want to deal with this, didn't want to talk about it. Yet Jess had a way of pressing him. "We're not involved, and we're not going to be. But if you think my friendship with Summer is going to pose a problem in the way I run this hospital…"

Jess thrust out his palm to defuse what seemed to be an impending argument. "I just asked if you were bringing Summer to the Equus Charity Ball this Friday night. Rafe wanted me to tell you that Myra will be watching the children up at the mansion. And Edie will be there, helping out, since she's just had the baby and doesn't want to go out of the house quite so soon. Thought Summer would be relieved to hear that, in case she hadn't made arrangements for Alyssa. Or you, for Chris."

"Nice to know, and I'll pass that along to

Summer. But I haven't asked her. Haven't even mentioned it to her."

Jess raised his eyebrows. "I assumed you would."

"No assumptions. We're friends, colleagues." He shrugged, almost too exaggeratedly, like he was trying too hard to make his point. "That's all there is to it, OK?"

Jess arched his eyebrows, but kept a straight face. "OK. My mistake. Though I'm not the only one making that assumption. And don't get me wrong, Rick. I'm not trying to start rumors or anything, but there are some people around here who are wondering what's going on between you two. You and Summer together, you have that… *look*." He drew in a stiff breath, then pushed himself out of the chair across the desk from Rick and headed toward the door. "Anyway, the invitation stands. Bring the kids up to the mansion if you want to. And so you won't think I'm trying to *push* you into something, I'll go extend the same invitation to Summer, and you both can decide if you want to come together or separately. However the two of you work it out is up to you."

"We're not a couple," Rick insisted once more, this time a bit grumpily, before Jess stepped into the hall.

"And I never said you were. But, damn, you're so defensive about it, that's what everybody's going to think if you're not careful. You know what they say about protesting too much!"

What everybody was going to think... Rick reared back in his chair to ponder that, but was cut short by a minor emergency in the ER. Food poisoning, multiple cases coming in from the Ladies' Garden Society. Refreshments gone bad at their monthly meeting. Nobody serious, but everybody with miserable symptoms. And that's what took up all his thoughts for the next two hours, except for those unguarded moments when Summer managed to slip in there somewhere between one lady's nausea and another lady's chills. Truth was, if he allowed himself a *type*, Summer would be it. But he simply couldn't allow himself a type because he didn't trust his judgement. The first time it had involved only him. Next time Chris would be a part of whatever decision he made, and that's what made the difference. It's what also stopped him cold in his tracks because if he did happen to get involved with Summer, and it turned out they didn't work as a couple, all he could see coming out of that was a huge disaster. His, hers…their children's.

Nope, not worth it. But damn it to hell, anyway!

"Are you going?" Summer asked him. She was crawling around an overgrown weed patch outside the hospital, taking measurements and snapping digital photos.

"Probably. As I'm involved with the foundation."

Looking up, she visored her eyes from the sun. "And you're leaving Chris with Myra? Because I was thinking that if I do go, I'd leave Alyssa there, too." Grace talked about the ball months ago, and it sounded lovely. But affairs such as that were meant to be shared with someone else. It was no fun going alone so she hadn't given it much thought. Not until now, anyway.

"You're not sure you're going?" Rick asked.

Summer shrugged. "I really have a lot of work to do. You know, plans for the pediatric ward."

"Which you shouldn't hide behind, Summer. You work hard for the foundation, you deserve the night."

"Except I'm not a big fan of huge parties. In the past, when I've been forced to go to one, I've always been the person hiding behind the potted palm, sipping my champagne alone, trying, at all costs, to avoid conversation." Pushing herself up, she stood, then brushed the dirt off the knees of her pants.

He chuckled. "So there's an antisocial side to you?"

She gestured an inch with her fingers. "Just a little one. And it only comes out during large parties."

"What if I stood in for that potted palm? Let you hide behind me while you sip your champagne?"

Out of nowhere, her heart skipped a beat. Was he really asking her out? "Then I'd be isolating you."

"That's assuming I don't want to be isolated. Maybe I do. Maybe I'd love to have a reason to stand off on the sidelines."

"Are you saying that to put me at ease, or do you really mean it?"

He smiled. "Attending social events goes along with my job as chief of staff. My personal preference is grabbing a pizza with Chris."

"So maybe we should do pizza instead."

"Or schedule time for the four of us to have pizza."

"We can do that, but that's not going to solve what we should do about the charity ball."

"We could get dressed up and go." He smiled. "Separately together, if that makes you feel any better."

"Separately together?"

"You know, both of us show up, wave at each other from across the room, know that we're there for each other if we need a crutch or a potted palm."

"That's an interesting concept, going as props, not dates."

He arched playful eyebrows. "No pressure, no obligation when you're a prop."

And very, very safe. That, above all else, was what she wanted. Because anything that could be construed as a date with Rick, well…she'd had the fantasy about what that could be like. Magical. Amazing. The moments fond sighs were made of. And that's all she'd get. "Sounds good to me."

"Good, then I'll meet you at the first potted palm to the right of the entrance."

"Lovely," she said, somehow wishing he'd argue her into a real date, or at least try a little harder. Oh, well. He was only giving her what she'd asked for. So there was no arguing about that, was there?

"Now, can you tell me what the hell you're doing out here, crawling around in the dirt, taking pictures?"

"It's about a fairy garden. You remember the ladies from the Garden Society…the ones who are sprawled all over the emergency department right now?"

"All of them a subtle shade of green?"

"Well, they've volunteered to create a fairy garden for Pediatrics. I thought this space would be lovely. And they're going to start the transformation just as soon as you can fix them up and send them on their way. So I figured I'd get measurements and photos ready for them before they leave."

Instead of replying, he just smiled. Then turned away.

As he did, Summer turned the other direction and headed back inside to clean up then check on Heather Anderson, and do another finger stick. On her way to the door, though, she had to resist the urge to turn back around and call out to Rick that she wanted to make their night at the Equus Charity Ball a real date. But she didn't. Common sense prevailed. Still, she was disappointed. But the thing was, being around Rick, with or without the potted palm, was getting difficult.

"A ball was Edie's idea, as Lilly Lake's way of thanking Grace for everything she did for the community. Grace loved her horses with a passion, and she would have loved the idea of a charity ball." Rick handed Summer a glass of champagne. They were definitely *not* hiding behind a potted palm. In fact, they were standing dead center in the stable, a place everybody passed whether they were going to the dance floor or on their way to the buffet. And they were standing close, touching shoulders, leaning into each other in order to hear over the noise of the crowd and the music. "I mean, all her charities are worthy, but this is the one that's involved so many of the people in Lilly Lake, brought us together as a community."

"It's a wonderful idea," Summer said, taking it all in. A charity ball in a horse stable…a romantic notion, she thought. While it wasn't fancy, the way a typical ball would be fancy, it was certainly lovely. Johnny Redmond had done a wonderful job of turning a stable into a ballroom, and even though there were no crystal chandeliers and showy floral arrangements, he'd cleaned the place until it was spotless, braided ribbons through the horses' manes, and adorned each stall door with bows to match the ribbons of the horse inside. In addition, there was a catered buffet, fit for royalty, being served in a white, high-peaked tent outside the main stable door, as well as a fully stocked bar under a canopy just across the entry path—all of it donated by local establishments wanting to do their part. Inside the stable a small orchestra tucked away at the end was playing light jazz, while several formally clad couples danced on an oak floor laid especially for the ball.

Sure, Summer had been to fancier soirées, danced to larger orchestras, smelled the fragrance of gardenias adorning massive floral displays, but decorated horse stalls and a temporary dance floor were nice and oddly fitting for the occasion. This was all about an outpouring of love from the town.

"And it's absolutely lovely, Rick," Summer said, tipping the champagne flute to her lips. A splash of reality blended with fairy-tale charm. "Every bit of it. Were you the organizer?"

"One of many. I think this ball will become part of Lilly Lake's texture, something everyone will look forward to each year. After all, it's something that defines us. A few horses to care for, and we all become united in something that's important." He smiled. "There's a lesson to be learned there, I suppose. At least one for me, because I spent a good part of my younger life not fitting in here. Besides that, a ball is the only time you're going to see some of Lilly Lake's men in tuxedos."

It was hard imagining Rick not fitting in. He was such a natural, people responded so easily to him. But she'd heard the stories, knew the circumstances, and could almost picture the little boy standing on the outside, looking in. Something she feared for Alyssa, with the way they had to live.

"It is important. Caring for another human being who needs help, or an animal…that's really all there is, you know. All we're supposed to do, and I think Grace knew that differently, or deeper than most people. And the men do look very handsome in their tuxedos." She took a quick appraisal of Rick, who was stunning with his black tux against his dark skin and black hair. If a man could be described as beautiful, then Rick was a beautiful man, breathtakingly so this evening. "Especially you, Rick. It suits you."

"Well, I prefer jeans or scrubs…"

Two other stunning images of him. Truth was, Rick was handsome in the rough *or* polished. No denying it.

"But once a year…" He shrugged. Smiled.

Gestured to his tuxedo. "For Grace. And you, Summer…you look amazing. Beautiful."

She was flattered. But, really, amazing and beautiful in her simple black dress, *sans* adornment? Not so much. In fact, she was probably the most understated woman there. Of course, she didn't have a very elaborate wardrobe these days. She'd left it behind, like she had everything else but the basics, and now she really didn't want to duplicate it, not in full, not even in part. Yet the simple black dress…nothing ostentatious, nothing that stood out. It worked.

"In case you hadn't noticed it, you're turning the heads of every man at the ball."

Probably because she'd gained a few *happy* pounds since she'd moved to Lilly Lake, transforming her from nervously skinny to her ideal weight. And the dress had been bought during her nervously skinny days, meaning that now she filled it out a little more amply than she'd expected. So if she was turning a few heads, it was, in all likelihood, because as her dress hugged her curves a little tighter than it should, it also pulled up a little shorter. Not a bad look, she had to admit. And turning a few heads wasn't exactly shabby. Most of all, she liked the way Rick looked at her. It had been a long, long time since she'd seen that kind of admiration in a man's eyes and tonight it made her feel…sexy. Appreciated.

"Thank you," she said.

Rick held up his champagne glass in tribute. "No. Thank you!"

Maybe it was the champagne on an empty stomach, maybe it was simply the ambience, but suddenly, impulsively, she asked, "What does it take to get one of these handsome men to ask a lady to dance?"

"Normally, I'd say something like a come-hither glance, but in your case…" he held out his hand to her "…no glance necessary. Would you care to accompany me to the dance floor, Nurse Adair?"

"I'd be honored, Dr Navarro."

Rick took Summer's hand and led her through the various groups of people, then stopped just at the edge of the dance floor. "Confession time. I'm not very good at this. Haven't had much cause for dancing in my life, so if you still want to take a chance with me, make sure you watch out for your toes."

"Maybe I should have worn steel-toed slings."

"Or your riding boots."

"Now, that's a look." She glanced down at her open toes, then back up at him. "Doesn't matter. I know a good doctor who can fix broken toes. So…"

The first moment was awkward, trying to fit body to body, but it took only seconds for Summer to slip into a natural place with Rick, with his hand sliding intimately around her waist then coming to rest just a fraction below it, while her head tilted to his shoulder, but only slightly.

At first they stood in place, swaying to the music, maybe too caught up in the feel of their bodies pressed together to risk losing that closeness. Then, as they noticed that other couples were dancing around them, they, likewise, stepped into the dance. Only their dance was not active, not one involved in the steps or in swirling around the floor. It was about that primal need to stay together, to not lose that familiarity. It was about *not* finding their place in the dance so much as finding their place in each other.

They didn't speak during that five-minute interlude, neither did they gaze longingly into each other's eyes. Rather, they simply moved to the underlying carnal beat of the music. It was pure, it was seductive and when it ended Summer was so weak in the knees she wasn't sure she could walk off the dance floor without being carried. "No broken toes," she murmured, clinging to Rick and feeling sad that the little interlude had ended.

"Maybe after a walk in the moonlight, we'll try another dance and go for two in a row without an injury. Care to accompany me outside?"

She'd accepted his pseudo-invitation to the ball with trepidation, yet now she was glad she'd come. Rick was a perfect gentleman, a perfect date even though, technically speaking, this wasn't a date. Just two unattached colleagues getting together to avoid looking pathetically alone. But she *was* pathetically alone, and that was something she couldn't disregard, not even as she strolled along the garden path in the moonlight, on Rick's arm. This was an illusion.

Or a momentary diversion. In her real life, she didn't get to have any of it.

"Where do you find time for doing so many things, Rick?" she asked, as he showed her to a marble bench under a wisteria canopy. "The hospital, the Gracie Foundation, raising Chris… you're a busy man."

Taking a seat next to her, he chuckled. "A busy man who can get by on very little sleep."

"Do you ever find time for yourself?"

"Everything I do is for myself. All of it makes my unglamorous life better."

"Depends on your definition of glamorous, I suppose, because nothing about your life seems unglamorous to me. Everything you do is for someone else, though. What I want to know is, do you ever just go off by yourself for a little while, to read, or meditate? Or get involved in something you enjoy just for the sake of enjoyment, like ride out to your boulder to admire the view? Maybe even go out on a date without taking Chris along?" OK, so this was a little fact-finding expedition, she'd admit that. And maybe she was just beating her head against the wall or opening herself to more pain, but while she was pretty sure Rick didn't date, she wanted to know.

"OK, I'll admit it. There's not a lot of time left over for me. But I really don't need to be involved socially. Don't need to be alone either. Truth is, with a couple of gaps here and there, I'm pretty contented with my life the way it is."

Meaning he didn't date. It was a relief, yet worthless to know because it didn't change her situation one way or the other. "I'd like to be contented. So far, that hasn't worked out for me, but I think it's my dream. You know, find my ideal situation, make Alyssa happy there, then simply exist."

"This isn't it?"

Summer drew in a deep breath. "Maybe. There are some days when I really hope so, but there are even more days when I just don't know." Suddenly she tensed up. She was saying too much, telling Rick things that could lead to questions she wouldn't answer. Rick was so easy to talk to, though. So easy to be around. Consequently, Summer physically bit down on her lip to stop herself from saying something she'd regret, because regrets meant she'd have to run away again and this time, she really, truly wanted to stay.

"You chilly?" he asked, putting his arm around her shoulders. "Would you like my jacket?"

"Not chilly," she said, *so* loving the feel of him, not wanting him to withdraw it just yet. Her natural inclination would have been to rest her head on his shoulder, then to sit there quietly, intimately, and let the night slip away while they didn't notice. But she couldn't. Just this once, though, she didn't want to be on her guard. Didn't want her outside world invading this. So she did allow her head to fall onto his shoulder, did allow his arm to stay around her. "Just...taking it all in." And wishing for a fairy-tale ending.

"Would you care to dance again?" he asked her.

"I hate to leave the garden," she confessed.

"We don't have to. Can you hear the music?"

She could. The strains of the orchestra were carrying on the night breeze, mingling with the call of the bullfrog and the laughter of the guests. But dancing in the moonlight seemed so...romantic. It scared her a little when she decided to decline. And scared her even more when Rick stood, then extended his hand to her, and she took it.

"One night," she whispered, as *both* his arms slipped around her this time, and both her hands slipped around his neck. Not the traditional dance form, the formal one reserved for charity balls and respectable public appearance, but the form of lovers on the verge of promises for more to come after the dance.

"What?" he asked.

"I said it's a lovely night." And it was, as the music swept them into each other, intimately so. Only this time they didn't have to move about the dance floor. Didn't have to make way to let others dance around them. This time they stood in place, body pressed to body, swaying to the rhythm. For now the moment was theirs. They owned the night and existed inside it as lovers. But then the music stopped, and she still clung to Rick, didn't want to let go. Couldn't let go for once she did, it would all be over. So, for a moment, they remained pressed together, still swaying to their own music. Then, gently, Rick placed his thumb under her chin and tipped her head up.

"You are so beautiful," he murmured, as his lips met hers.

She wanted that kiss. Snuggled into it. Let herself go and allowed it to ooze through her like melted chocolate. For only a moment, though. Because, as he pressed for more, and she craved more, she caught herself in time. Pushed herself back from him. "I…um…I need to go," she said, her voice on the edge of panic.

"Why?"

"We… I can't do this, Rick. It's a beautiful evening, you're a wonderful man, but it's too much. Too complicated." *What was she doing?* This was crazy. She knew better.

"Complications can be undone, Summer. If you want them to be."

She laughed, but sadly. "It's not always that easy."

"Could be, if you'd let somebody get close to you."

If only she could. But she couldn't. And the lovely moment had escaped. No fairy-tale endings here. "Thank you for the dance, Rick. You underestimate yourself. My toes were never in danger." But her heart was. Unlike Rick or Rafe or Jess, who could fix broken toes, there was nobody who could fix her heart if it broke. And if she allowed herself another moment with Rick, it would surely break.

CHAPTER SEVEN

ONE night after the ball, and she was still all jitters. If she hadn't already promised Alyssa this pizza date, she'd be home, playing games with her or reading her a story. But this was their date for four, and there was safety in numbers. Thank God for that. "Are you sure it's OK for her to be up at the window?" she asked, as her jitters over Rick turned into the normal in public jitters she had every time she and Alyssa stepped out of their…out of *her* comfort zone.

"She's fine up there," Rick said, as he showed Summer to a table. "The kids love it. It gives them a great view of the pizzas being made."

She craned her neck to keep an eye on Alyssa, as she couldn't see her daughter well enough from that vantage point. But the restaurant was crowded and they had been lucky to get a table. The hostess said another might not be available for an hour, so this was it. And she didn't like it. There was no way to reposition herself, or the table, in order to keep a better eye on her daughter and a good case of panic was already overtaking everyday jitters. "I think maybe I'll go and join them," she said, and started to stand. But Rick laid a gentle hand on hers, stopping her.

"You need to relax, Summer. I know you're trying to be a good mom, but Alyssa has to have some breathing space. There's a fine line between mothering and smothering."

That was true, and she did cross over that line too often. Still, not being able to see Alyssa was ruining her evening and she couldn't help it. So she pulled her hand away from Rick's and stood all the way up. "Being protective isn't smothering. And she's four, Rick. Smothering at that age isn't a bad thing."

But apparently Alyssa thought it was, because once Summer reached the pizza window, her daughter totally ignored her. Didn't turn around when Summer said her name, didn't respond when Summer asked her if she wanted to come back to the table and help order the pizza. So, at Alyssa's tender age, was she already building up some resentment to the smothering? Or was this her daughter's attempt to assert some independence by telling her mother she wasn't necessary all the time?

Perplexed, maybe even a little hurt, these were questions Summer contemplated all the way back to the table, which Rick had switched to one in much closer proximity to the pizza window. "How'd you manage that?" she asked him, glad of the better vantage.

A grin crossed his face. "Cooperative patient."

"Thank you, Rick," she said, dropping down into her seat, relieved she had a perfect view of her daughter now. "I know I seem too protective, but..."

"Nothing wrong with being a good mother."

"Maybe there is. I think Alyssa's beginning to resent my...shall we call it closeness? I saw it today at the day-care center, when she didn't want to be interrupted while she was playing. And even now, at the pizza window, she totally ignored me."

"She's growing up. They all do it."

"I know, and I want to stop it."

Rick chuckled. "I loved Chris while he was going through his terrible twos. A lot of people told me that would be the worse, but for me it was exciting. Then he grew up a little more, progressed a little more, and I hated it because I missed the way he'd been. That was my insecurity, though. You know, growing up, growing distant, not being needed any longer. Or, at least, not being needed quite so much. I mean, he's only six, and I already get depressed when I think how soon he'll be gone…off to college, off to his own life, wife, kids… But it's inevitable, and all I can do is enjoy what I have right now, and look forward to what I'll have tomorrow, rather than dreading it. And I really have to work at it."

"So there's no magical prescription for stopping the changes?" she asked, her total focus on Alyssa, who was laughing and having the time of her life…*without her.*

"If only we could do that. But the thing I've discovered is that as Chris changes…grows, it's all good, and it broadens my horizons as much as it does his because it gives me a different outlook on life, lets me experience things in a way I never would otherwise. Pizza, for instance. Before Chris, I could take it or leave it. It was food, pretty much the same as everything else I ate. No big deal. But my son changed all that for me, made me see the beauty in a simple thing—pizza dough, tomato sauce, a few veggies, a little meat. It's an amazing work of art the way it all goes together, and I know that because..." He gestured to the kids. "Look at how they're watching the process, so engrossed in the little things going on. To them it's exciting, a learning process. Makes you rethink a lot of things when you see them through your child's eyes for the first time. That's where the beauty is, Summer. Not in the pizza so much as it is in watching them watch the process. Watching them...grow."

What Rick said was true, but difficult. She wanted to see the changes in Alyssa as an exciting process, but there was so much of her that didn't want to let go. "I really didn't want to do this tonight, and I came up with about a dozen reasons to beg off. I know my anxieties are a little overbearing at times, but I like my security, like to keep myself in a place where I can control...everything. You're a smart man, Rick Navarro," she said, finally relaxing back into her chair. "I'm glad I listen to you."

"Not smart so much as I'm just able to figure it out with an *aha* snap of my fingers and a light bulb going on over my head once I've made the mistake. What I realized in one of those *aha* moments, though, was that while I have to think about my son's future, my greatest challenge is getting us through today before I can worry about tomorrow. If I don't, then I miss today. So I've let up."

Getting Alyssa and her through the day… She could do that. But not without thinking about Cameron, not without plotting what she'd do if he suddenly appeared. No aha moments, because everything had to be planned, then watched over carefully. And now she was on edge again, thinking about all the uncertainties in her life yet fighting not to show it. "If I could ask you something personal, does Chris's mother pose some kind of threat to the way you're raising him? I know she gave him up, but does she ever want any involvement?"

"No. When she walked away, she walked away from everything. Didn't want to know."

If only Cameron had been the same.

"Why? Does your ex want to hang on?"

She shook her head, even though it was a lie. "We severed ties pretty easily." And the lies kept compounding.

"I know your ex wasn't good for you, otherwise you'd still be with him. But was he a good father to Alyssa?"

No, she wanted to say. Wanted to scream. But she deferred to her usual position, the one that kept her safe. "He's a busy man, no time for a family. Doesn't want to make time." Same old tired lie, or delusion. It came almost naturally now, she'd told it so many times.

"So, does he have partial custody?"

"No," she lied. Truth was, she shared custody with Cameron. Which was why she'd had to run. She would never...*never* trust her daughter with that man and sharing custody meant weekend visits and every other holiday, plus a night or two a week. "He was agreeable," she said, wishing she'd never gone this far with Rick because he was an honorable man. One who would never understand the kinds of things she'd done to get away, to survive. More than that, he would never understand why yet another person in his life chose to deceive him. But it was a choice she had to make, to protect Alyssa, even to protect Rick. "We've worked things out." Lie upon lie. She hated it, hated that Cameron had forced her into this situation.

"Look, it's time to think pizza, OK? I know two kids who are going to come back to the table pretty hungry." She glanced over Alyssa and Chris, with their faces pressed to the window, still watching the pizza spinner do his thing. To the casual observer, she and Rick, Alyssa and Chris…they looked like any other family sitting in Mama Rosa's dining room. Mom, dad, two kids…

"Pepperoni and lots of cheese," he said.

"Mushrooms and olives. Extra-thick crust. And green peppers."

"Chris hates green peppers, but he can pick them off."

They both decided against the onions when the waitress took the order, and they kept the conversation focused on pizza preferences for the next couple of minutes, both of them agreeing that their kids would eat pizza every day of the week, and both of them trying to get over that awkward hurdle from bad marriages to better places with trivial banter. "Well, it's too bad we have to grow up and deal with eating what's good for you more than eating what you want," Summer finally said, as the chat between them started to wane. She didn't want it to, didn't want it to go back to Cameron or anything else that would take away from the evening they were having now, as she was actually beginning to let down some, beginning to enjoy herself. "Me, I'd have popcorn every day of the week. Popcorn dripping with butter. And lots of salt. Oh, and a cola to go with it…not a diet cola either. A regular one, with sugar. That's my idea of a perfect meal."

Rick chuckled. "Hamburgers for me, with French fries. Maybe not every day, but every other day would suit me."

"So we can't fault the kids for their passion for pizza, can we?"

"No, we can't fault them, but we can envy them for a little while since it won't be all that long before they're sucked into eating what's good for them and not what they want, like we were at some point in our lives…for me, after college when I had to take off twenty pounds of college junk food fat." He glanced back over at the kids, then blinked and took a second look. Immediately, he scooted to the edge of his seat. "Um, I'll be back in a second," he said, pushing himself off the booth bench.

Summer beat him to it, though, because as Rick was beginning to notice that Chris was standing alone at the pizza window, she'd already spotted that very same thing and was propelling herself into instant action. "Alyssa!" she shouted above the racket of the other families in the restaurant. "Mommy can't see you, sweetheart. Where are you, Alyssa?"

"She probably got swallowed up in the crowd," Rick said, staying right at her side as she shot across the restaurant, shoving through the masses of children and adults in line at the salad bar, standing at the pizza window or simply mingling.

"I should have never done this," Summer cried. "I knew better. Knew it was a bad idea… Alyssa, where are you, sweetheart? Please, Alyssa, tell Mommy where you are."

Rick caught up to Chris who, apparently, hadn't noticed that his little companion had disappeared. "Did you see where she went?" he asked, trying to remain calm.

Chris shook his head and his eyes welled with tears. "She was right here. I didn't know..."

"It's OK, sport. Maybe she just went to the bathroom." He looked in that direction, only to see Summer emerge from there, looking more frantic than ever. What he was witnessing was a parent's worse nightmare, and he couldn't even begin to imagine what Summer was feeling. But extending his hand to Chris, then taking hold and holding on for dear life, he realized he *could* imagine. And that's when he called...his brothers.

"She's not here," Summer said moments later. "Rick, I've looked everywhere, and..." She glanced down at Chris, saw the tears streaming down his cheeks. "Maybe you should take him home," she said. "He's scared to death and he doesn't need to be here for this."

"Rafe and Jess are on their way. Julie said she'd come and get Chris if we need her to."

Summer nodded, forced a weak smile. "I appreciate it, but I can't wait for them. I'm going out to the parking lot. Maybe she wandered outside."

"I'll call the police…"

"No!" she choked. "Don't do that. Please, not yet."

What he was seeing now was a different kind of panic, one he didn't understand. "OK, not yet. But, Summer, if we don't find her soon…"

She regrouped, swallowed back the sob wanting to escape her. "We're going to find her, Rick. I'm sure she simply got turned around. So, please, no police, not yet…"

He agreed reluctantly, but didn't like it. When your child was in jeopardy, nothing was enough. And he did wonder now about Summer's motives, and even her over-protectiveness. He agreed, though. But not for long. Damn, his gut *and his heart* hurt for Summer in ways he could have never expected.

Ten minutes into the frantic search and there was still no sign of Alyssa. Jess and Rafe were already on the scene, checking adjacent buildings, while Rick searched the pizza parlor, top to bottom. Summer's panic had given way to cold numbness, and then to single-minded thinking. *She had to find her daughter.* That was her only focus so, to that end, she was crawling around on her hands and knees on the dirty asphalt parking lot, tearing her linen pants, scraping her knees and using her medical penlight to look underneath each and every car parked there. Finding only crushed soda cans and old candy wrappers, trying not to think the one thought that would make her curl up into a fetal position and cry. No, she couldn't...*wouldn't* think that Cameron had taken Alyssa because Alyssa could be only a heartbeat away, waiting to be found.

Or miles from here by now, on a road to a place she might never find.

"Alyssa," she called, her frantic edge rising with each passing second. "Please, sweetheart. Mommy wants to see you. Can you tell Mommy where you are?"

"Summer?" Rick shouted from somewhere closer to the building.

"I can't find her," Summer shouted back. "I've looked under every car out here, and she's not..." Her voice caught. She fought back the tears and tried to brace herself to keep looking. But nearly twenty minutes had elapsed now, and she knew it was time to do more. Time to destroy everything she'd worked so hard toward for the sake of finding her daughter. "We should call the police now," she said, as the numbness in her grew even more pervasive.

Rick ran to Summer's side, immediately dropping to his hands and knees. "We found her. She was in the kitchen. She'd gone into the pantry to see if she could find the ingredients to help make pizza dough, and shut the door behind her." He chuckled. "Couldn't reach the doorknob to get out, so she huddled up in the back, in the dark, and waited. Then fell asleep. But she's fine, Summer. Covered head to toe with flour, but no worse for wear."

"You're laughing?" Summer sputtered, pushing herself to a standing position then bending to dust off her soiled knees. "How can you do that? My daughter went missing, Rick, and you're laughing about it, saying she's no worse for the…?" Her voice broke and tears finally slid down her cheeks.

Rick stood up, tried to calm her by pulling her into his arms, but she shoved him back…hard.

"I'm not laughing, Summer. I was scared just like you were. So were Rafe and Jess. But she's fine. Everything's fine and that's all we need to think about right now."

"No, it's not. Don't you understand? There's nothing *fine* here. Nothing! And there are too many things to think about, too many decisions I'm going to have to make because of this."

She turned, started to run toward the building, but Rick caught up with her and physically stopped her. Grabbed hold of her arm, then held her in place. "I don't know what the hell's going on with you, Summer, but there's something, and it's obvious you don't trust me enough to tell me. Whatever it is, leave it out here because Alyssa can't see you like this. You're almost hysterical, you're shaking. And mad at the world over something you're trying to fight alone. You also look like hell, and by the time you get to her you're going to have yourself worked into such an emotional state you'll scare her to death. Is that what you want?"

"Take your hands off me, Rick. I'm warning you…"

He shook his head. "Alyssa's having the time of

her life in there. She's happy. In her mind, she's just had a great adventure and she doesn't think she's done anything bad. Right now, Summer, she's playing up the part of a celebrity, helping to spin pizza in the window. More than anything, she's loving it. If you go in there the way you are now, and do what I think you're going to do…"

"The way I am now? Don't you understand? My daughter went missing. We were lucky that she was right here. But it could have turned out differently. She could have—"

"Not missing, Summer." he interrupted. "Alyssa was just temporarily somewhere you couldn't find her. And I know you were scared to death, but—"

"You don't know, Rick. You don't know *anything*," she nearly screamed. Then suddenly the fight went out of her. The fight, the wind, the will to do anything more than take her daughter and disappear again. It wasn't working out for them here in Lilly Lake. She'd become too settled, too happy. Too comfortable. "Look, I may have overreacted. But that's who I am, what I do. I protect my daughter, or I'm supposed to protect my daughter, but I didn't, and there's no excuse for that."

"You blinked, Summer. That's all you did. You blinked, and she got away. That doesn't make you a bad mother. It makes you…human, like the rest of us."

"Well, that's not good enough. I have to be better, be more diligent. I have to pay more attention."

"Because you're a single parent, and you have to try harder? I'm a single parent too, Summer. My mother was a single parent. So I know something about this."

"In your own circumstances maybe. But you don't know what it's like in mine," she said again, only this time her voice was filled with overwhelming sadness. In her heart of hearts she knew Rick was right…under normal circumstances. And she'd desperately wanted those normal circumstances in her own life, which was why she'd let herself get distracted, get caught up in pretending she was like every other mother in Mama Rosa's. Just part of one big, happy family. For a moment, somewhere between the discussion of green peppers and onions, she'd actually let herself believe she and Alyssa could actually have it all.

Well, they couldn't. And now they couldn't even have Lilly Lake. This time, though, they wouldn't be running away from Cameron. They'd be running away from her hopes and dreams, and that's what hurt. Because she'd slipped, and actually let herself believe she could have them.

Steadying herself with a deep breath, Summer squared her shoulders and braced to face Rick. "Look, Rick. I can't keep that job as head nurse in Pediatrics. I'm sorry, but it won't work out. I'll stay there temporarily, long enough for you to find someone else to take over. But it's not going to be me. I can't…no, I won't leave my daughter in day care even if it's only down the hall from my office."

"You're quitting because you lost sight of your daughter for a moment?" He shook his head, then finally released his grip on Summer and stepped back. "I put myself in that same position, thought about what I'd do, or how I'd respond if Chris went missing. It's a horrible thing, and I understand that you're still suffering the aftermath of what could have been the worst thing that might ever happen to a parent. But to quit your job because of it?"

"We all do what we have to do. I have to take better care of my daughter. That's all my life is about."

"Why, Summer? I'm not talking about why you have to take better care of Alyssa, because in my opinion you do a pretty damn fine job of it. But why are you overreacting by quitting? It doesn't make any sense, especially as you can see her any time you want during the day."

"It doesn't have to make sense to you. Nothing I do has to." But she was sad. She'd thought she'd found the perfect situation. All she'd found, though, was something she'd never have, and it was powerful enough to pull her away from the only thing she really had to do. Rick distracted her. The view of what she wanted with him distracted her. Well, never again. "Look, I'm going to go and get my daughter now, and take her home. And if you wish, I'll start posting ads for my replacement first thing tomorrow morning."

"You're not even going to let her stay and eat the pizza she's made?"

She wanted to. She desperately wanted to. But that was part of a normal life she didn't get to have. Angry tears squeezed from her eyes as she made her way back into Mama Rosa's, then stood for a moment, looking in the pizza window, watching her daughter having so much fun. The smile on Alyssa's face, her laughter, the way she was playing to the crowd watching her... Summer didn't like the world she was forced to dwell in. But there would be hell to pay if, or when, Cameron really did catch up with her. That knowledge was always with her, the constant reminder that she had to be diligent. Which was why they'd walk away from this life, start over, and never look back.

Yet as Rick walked into Mama Rosa's, then stood in the doorway, not coming any closer to her, she did look back...at him. When she did, her heart shattered.

CHAPTER EIGHT

IT WAS the first ever circus day in the pediatric ward. Not the kind of circus with live animals, although she'd hoped to introduce pony rides into the mix someday, but today there were magicians and jugglers, a couple of friendly clowns, balloons, and some congenial music from a senior citizens' orchestra consisting of three violins, a clarinet, a piccolo, some drums and a tuba. It was an interesting blend, to be sure, and the children were having the time of their lives, watching or participating.

Had it only been a week since that night at Mama Rosa's? It had gone by in a whirlwind, trying to get things ready for her replacement, trying to get circus day organized for the children as word was already out and the children were looking forward to it. Summer was pleased with the overall results. Snacks prepared with each child's dietary needs were being passed around by kitchen volunteers, parents had taken time off from work to come and assist with games, medical staff members were sneaking in wherever they could to be a part of this extravaganza, and all Summer could think was that she wouldn't be here next time circus day rolled around. She was sorry about that because it was her brainchild, getting the children involved in something other than their normal hospital routine and various medical conditions. Happiness and laughter contributed to healing, and if the expressions on the children's faces meant anything, each and every one of her sixteen pediatric patients was healing in some way right now by being part of this.

Circus day had been conceived as a monthly affair, along with picnic day, magic day, movie day and storytelling day. Originally, she'd hope to initiate some kind of special day once, maybe twice each week. So far, only circus day was in the carrying-out stage and she desperately hoped that the next nurse in charge would follow up where she would be leaving off, maybe even add a few other days she hadn't yet thought about.

Oh, well. She'd probably never know the final

outcome of her idea, which was making her feel pretty bleak, even though she was smiling through it and, presently, trying to twist a balloon into the shape of a poodle for one of the little girls, Amy Cavanaugh. Her dog, as it turned out, looked more like an abstract octopus, but Amy was pleased with it.

"You're really going to leave all this?" Rick whispered in her ear. "Walk away from what you've created?"

She spun to face him. "I need something else, and it's not like I'm deserting it. What I've done here will be simple enough to carry on with someone else."

"So why don't I believe what you're telling me? Because I thought you were happy here, Summer. I thought you liked raising Alyssa here."

Summer twisted off the section that was the dog's tail then handed the balloon to Amy, who, beaming, showed it to her parents. "You can believe whatever you want," she whispered back to Rick, then pointed to the door leading to the hall. "If you want to talk, that's fine. But not around the children."

Shrugging, he followed her to the hall, where several staff members were loitering, watching the circus through the pediatric ward window. So Summer continued on down the hall, and eventually outside, to the beginnings of the fairy-tale garden. "OK, so let me have it," she snapped, once the door shut behind Rick.

"Have what?"

"You're angry. I get it. I accepted the job, you made certain concessions in order to convince me to take it, and now, before I've barely started, I'm handing it back to you. It's been a whole week since I told you I had to leave here, and you haven't said a thing. Not one word. It's like I never said I was quitting. Or if you didn't acknowledge it, it wouldn't happen. But it's going to happen, Rick. I'm already making enquiries into other job options." She wasn't, but she didn't want him to know that.

"If you want to know the truth, I don't have anything in writing from you. No letter of resignation, not even a note, or an e-mail. Hospital protocol dictates that I need to have something in writing. So, until I do, you're not *officially* quitting."

"You've got to be kidding. I told you—"

"Telling doesn't mean anything. A lot of people say a lot of things they don't mean, then take them back."

"I didn't take anything back. What I said—"

"I'm forgetful," he interrupted.

"Forgetful?" She started to walk around him in a circle—a slow, deliberate circle. He circled along with her but in place so to always face her. Kept up with her, was never out of direct eye contact, as she circled like a predatory wildcat. "Since when are you forgetful?" she finally questioned after several long, silent moments of posturing.

A challenging smile slid over his face. "When I want to be. When not remembering something I don't want to benefits whatever I want it to benefit. In this case, the hospital. *And me.*"

Still circling, her eyes flashed. "But I could walk away. Right now. This very instant. Leave you without a written notice, clear out my office, walk through the front door and never come back." Not that she would since she'd given her word to stay until she was replaced. In theory, though, she could.

"On circus day?" He pointed in the window. "Look what you've done here, Summer. Little Amy Cavanaugh in there had chemotherapy yesterday for her leukemia. Normally the day after her treatment she's weak, feels like hell, can't get out of bed. But she's doing a ring toss with that…that clown. And laughing. And not feeling so out of place because she doesn't have any hair. Just look at her!" He took two steps forward, physically stopped Summer from her circling, and pointed her toward the window.

"That's what *you* did, Summer! You gave Amy a rare *day after*, something no one's done before. And that's why you're needed here. It's more than your ability as a nurse. You have the heart and soul this hospital needs. You know how to care for these kids in ways nobody else does. Sure, we can find another nurse to replace you, probably someone with good administrative skills who's equally good with patient care. We're growing, offering new programs. Lilly Lake is a beautiful area with amazing potential to turn itself into a resort area or something equally as nice. People want to work here now that the hospital is expanding and we're offering competitive and even better services than any of the other regional hospitals in the area.

"But the people I want working here are people like you, people who have a different vision for patient care, people who go beyond dispensing medicine and ordering tests and who understand what the human spirit needs in the whole healing process. People who know how to make a difference in Amy Cavanaugh's fight for her life. And that's a rare quality. I mean, circus day? Really? I'm a dad, love my son to pieces, consider myself a good, attentive parent. But circus day is something that would never have crossed my mind, and I don't want to lose the person whose mind it did cross. She's invaluable, and the things I need the most are the ones that can't be replaced by someone else."

Summer ran a hand through her hair. He didn't want to lose her...for the hospital, *not* for himself. It's what she wanted, of course. Exactly what she wanted. But sometimes she did wish that her knight in shining armor would come riding up and try rescuing her, even though she knew she really couldn't be rescued. One thing she'd learned, and learned well, thanks to Cameron, was that fairy tales were for fools. "You did fine before I came here," she said half-heartedly, wishing he could wager a winning argument against her and say something that would make it all right for her to stay. "You'll do fine when I leave."

"You're probably right on both counts. But I want to do better than fine, Summer. Fine isn't good enough any more."

"Because you've got something to prove to your brothers? Because you want to prove you're the best Corbett of all, even though the rest of the Corbetts don't know you're one of them? Is that what this is about, Rick?"

"It's about the hospital!" he snapped. "Only about the hospital. And I don't need to prove anything to Rafe and Jess."

"Don't you? I mean, you say your history with them is water under the bridge. Maybe you even believe that, or think if you say it often enough that will make it true. But you're still fighting against them, Rick. Not telling them something they have a right to know is fighting against them, whether or not you want to admit that. And I think that making this hospital bigger and better is another way of you trying to prove something to them. I don't mean this to be cruel either. But while you're trying to pick apart my reason for leaving, you really need to be examining your reasons for pretty much everything you do concerning Rafe and Jess. Including the hospital."

"You're way out of line here, Summer. Just because you know—"

"Know what?" She shook her head. "I don't know anything, Rick. If I did, I'd be settled somewhere, happy. But I'm not. And that's the only thing I know for sure. The rest of it…" Glancing in the window so she wouldn't have to look at Rick, she saw her daughter juggling three red sponge balls. Alyssa was laughing, looking so bright and happy playing with all the children in the ward, as well as the handful now enrolled in the day-care program, not at all aware that just outside her mother was planning on disrupting her life. Another instance, like at Mama Rosa's Pizza, where her daughter was moving forward in her own life. "I don't know what else to tell you, Rick. It's not working out for me here, and I don't know how to make it work."

"You own a house here. Doesn't that mean anything?"

It did. More than he could know. "No loss, no gain," she said, trying to sound unemotional. "I didn't buy it. So I'll deed it back to the Gracie Estate…" She forced a smile. "That would be you now, wouldn't it?"

He flinched at that, but didn't react. "So after you give it back, then what?"

She noticed that Rick ignored her last remark about being part owner of the Gracie Estate the way he ignored so much of what tormented him. It was unfortunate he did that, as Rick had so much to gain if he'd face the truth himself, then told his brothers. It was such an easy fix, one with the potential for a great outcome. Too bad she didn't have an easy fix available to her. "I've toyed with the idea of going someplace where it's warm all year long." Not true, though. Maybe Canada? It was a vast country, many places not highly populated, and so much of it remote. Somebody could get lost there pretty easily without too much effort. Besides that, she was a citizen, thanks to her mother—a little fact Cameron hadn't known, which meant he might not go looking for her there. "I'm not really fond of cold weather and snow, and Lilly Lake can have bad winters. I think Alyssa might like someplace near an ocean, and I could certainly use more sun." There she was, always setting up a deception, always trying to get someone to buy into the myths she'd become so good at telling. Another by-product of her marriage. The only way she knew how to survive. "Anyway, I've got prospects, and I'm weighing them right now."

"So, what would it take for me to persuade you to keep Lilly Lake on your list of prospects? Because if you'd like to have circus day or picnic day every day, I can arrange for it."

Summer smiled. It was a beautiful fantasy and as impractical as it would be to carry out, she loved him for offering it. "It's not like I'm leaving right away, Rick. I'll be here awhile longer. I'm not leaving you in the lurch."

"Aren't you, Summer? Because from where I'm watching this whole thing take place, that's exactly what I see. I depended on you and you're throwing that right back at me."

OK, maybe she was, and she understood why Rick was angry. But this was about Alyssa. *Only*

Alyssa. No, Cameron had never hit her, but the day Summer had taken her daughter and run she'd witnessed him raise his fist to Alyssa. Alyssa had been rambunctious, loud, playing with gusto, the way only a child her age could, and Cameron had been annoyed by it. He'd told Alyssa to be quiet, and she'd asked him why. *Why?* One simple word and Cameron snapped, raised his fist...

She'd run at her husband, literally lunged at him, knocking him down before he could land the blow. But the blow had landed anyway, then more blows, over and over, just not on Alyssa, thank God. Afterwards, he'd said he wouldn't have hit their daughter, and Summer didn't know if he would have *that time*. Maybe he would have, maybe he wouldn't have. It didn't really matter any more because that had been the day she'd come to terms with the fact that it was only a matter of time until he did hurt Alyssa, because hitting was what he did.

But worse than that, Alyssa had witnessed something she never should have seen, and the look on her daughter's face when she'd seen her father hit her mother...fear, confusion.

Something a mother could never forget. "We don't fit here like I'd hoped we would." She swallowed hard, trying to find a way to finish the lie. "Lilly Lake is nice enough, but Alyssa needs more than what she's going to get here."

"Really? You're going to use your daughter as your excuse?" Rick turned around to the window, and looked at several of the children, including Chris, playing in a circle with some of the others. They were watching Daisy, the clown magician, pluck a coin from behind one of the children's ear. "So tell me, what doesn't fit?" he asked, pointing to Alyssa. "What am I missing here, Summer? Because I'm trying hard to figure it out, and I'll be damned if I can."

She spun around, started to walk away. But Rick pulled her into his arms. "I… Please, don't do this," she begged, deliberately not looking at him as her voice caught in her throat and tears welled in her eyes.

"Are you crying? Someone who's looking forward to a new life shouldn't be crying, Summer." He brushed a tear from her cheek with his thumb. "I could help you, if you let me."

His voice was so gentle now, so full of compassion all she wanted to do was let him make it all right. But what he'd felt about his mother… that's what stopped her, as she couldn't bear him knowing that *she'd* stayed, too. Couldn't bear how he would feel about her then. "I'm just tired. I've been working a lot of hours lately, trying to get everything ready for the transition, for when I—"

"I don't want you to go, Summer. There's nothing else I can say. I *do not* want you to leave."

As a nurse? As something else? She wanted him to say it. Dear God, there were words she wanted to hear. But hearing them would only make it worse because his words wouldn't change anything. "You'll find another nurse. I've talked to some candidates—"

"Damn it, Summer! Don't you understand? This isn't about finding another nurse. It's about…you. And me. I thought we were getting close. Thought maybe we might—"

"No, don't. Please, don't. Because I…" Her voice caught in her throat for a second time, but this time it totally failed her. When she opened her mouth to speak, the words just wouldn't come. They were in her heart, but leaden. Her whole life, this was what she'd wanted. Someone like Rick. Lilly Lake. Her job. And here it was, everything she could have ever hoped for, all of it wanting to embrace her, yet she couldn't even reach out and touch it.

"OK," he continued, "I know I spout off about not wanting another relationship, about how once was enough and my life with Chris is all I want. Part of that's true. I do mean what I say because my first marriage was… When I met her, when I fell in love almost immediately, it happened so fast I don't even remember anything leading up to it. I promised myself I'd never do that again. Promised myself that someday, when Chris was older, if I wanted to get involved, I'd be careful. Slow. Then one day I saw you and… First sight, Summer. There I was again, falling in love at first sight. And scared to death of how that could affect Chris, because the first time I did that was such a disaster. But it was you, and you're…you're the only one."

No, not now! The words she wanted to hear, but too late. Much too late. Summer drew in a ragged breath and braced herself to do the hardest thing she'd ever done. "I think it's just that you empathize with me because I'm a single parent trying to raise a child just like you are. "

He laughed bitterly. "Well, I do have a knack for picking the ones who don't want me, don't I? Just look at you standing there with your whole long laundry list of ways to reject me. So, which one are we on now, Summer?"

She lifted her gaze to meet his, tried hard not to let her stare waver. "The one where I've never made myself available. In fact, I've been clear that my life is only about Alyssa and me, that I don't want anybody else bothering us."

"Have you, Summer? Because that's not what I've seen. In fact, every time I've looked at you, I see a woman who wants something else. She wants it so badly she aches, and if she says otherwise, she's lying…probably more to herself than to anyone else. Remember when you told me you could see it in my eyes? Well, I see it in yours. *You are lying, Summer.* Every last word, every last implication…all of it's a lie. You want to stay here, and build your life here, even if it's not with me. You do fit. But maybe it's me you're running from? Running from the way I feel about you? Have you seen that in my eyes, and that's what scaring you?"

His words stung. Every one of them. Because Rick was right. "When I was eight years old, there was a doll I wanted more than anything in the world. My mother and I would go to the mall, and I'd see it in the store window. It was like I was consumed. I had to have that doll, and I knew if I begged hard enough, and showed lots of patience, that I would get it. Well, weeks rolled into months and no doll. Then it was Christmas and I *knew* Santa would bring me that doll. I'd been a good girl, I'd obeyed my parents. Done all the things Santa expected of me, except he didn't bring me the doll. On Christmas morning, I ran down the stairs and ripped open every gift. I got socks and a nightgown. A new toothbrush. All practical things. So I spent the rest of the day being angry and grumpy because I didn't get what I wanted, and I knew my parents felt bad. But I didn't care because I wanted them to feel as miserable as I did.

"What I didn't know, or wasn't mature enough to understand was that both my parents were unemployed and struggling just to keep a roof over our heads. What *would* I understand, or even care about something like that? I wanted that damned doll." Thoughts of that day still made her cringe, as it had been the last Christmas she was to have with her parents. They were killed shortly after, and the rest of her childhood had been spent with her grandmother. "What I learned from that…it came to me in retrospect years later. My parents bought me practical things because I needed them. And it's the best they could do. But they also bought me one very inexpensive nurse's kit because they wanted me to have a toy…" She smiled at the memory. "It wasn't what I wanted but what I needed because I loved that toy, and it became the start of something I wanted *and* needed in my life. What I want now is Lilly Lake, but what I need is…" *Lilly Lake. Keeping Alyssa and herself safe. Rick…* "This isn't about you, or my feelings for you. I promise, Rick, it's not. It's about me trying to find what I need, and I never meant for it to hurt you."

"Maybe it's time to change your perspective. Think about something new to want, or something different to need."

That was her conflict now. She did want something new, need something new. And the pain involved in walking away from it was growing. The longer she stayed, the more this was going to hurt. "I have. And I'm leaving to go and look for it."

"Yet I still don't believe you."

"So that's where we have to leave it, Rick," she said, slapping at a stray tear sliding down her face.

"Well, for what it's worth, which doesn't seem to be much, I don't want you leaving, and that's not the doctor addressing the nurse. It's me asking you."

But would he still ask if he knew the truth? Maybe that, more than anything else, was what she couldn't face. Because she loved this man with all her heart, and to see the look on his face when she told him she was everything he'd been disappointed in… He hadn't dealt with it in his mother yet. Neither had he faced up to telling his brothers the truth. He didn't need another emotional burden and she came with more burden than Rick deserved. "Look, I have to get back to work," she finally managed to say as she broke away from his hold on her—his physical hold. She didn't have any idea what to do about breaking away from his emotional hold. Maybe she couldn't. Maybe it was incurable.

"Well, damn it anyway," Rick said to Will Brassard over the beer he'd been nursing for nearly half an hour. Brassard's Pub was a good place to forget your sorrows, the thing Rick was trying hard to do. And Will Brassard, the owner-bartender, who also served as chief of Lilly Lake's volunteer fire department, was a good listener. Open mind, closed mouth. That was all Rick wanted right now. "It's not like I was proposing or anything. In fact, we haven't even had a proper date. But I scare the hell out of her and I don't know why." He knocked back a swig, then clanked his mug down on the bar. "She's got a good job here. Lots of friends. I know she loves volunteering at the Gracie Foundation with the horses. And Alyssa is happy and well adjusted. Yet Summer insists they don't fit here, and I don't know what that means because everything I see looks like she does."

"Is this reaction coming from her boss, or from

someone else?" Will asked. He and Rick had been friends since school. Not best buddies, but close enough to be counted as solid. "And don't try kidding the bartender, Rick. I see all, know all…"

In spite of his sour mood, Rick chuckled. "If you want to know the honest truth, I don't know *who* it's coming from. Part of me is totally convinced I'm trying to persuade her to stay for the hospital."

"But the other part of you?"

"You mean the bigger part?"

"I mean the part that knows the honest truth, even though he's not willing to admit it yet. The same thing you're accusing Summer of, by the way."

Rick rubbed his forehead and shut his eyes. It wasn't so much he was trying to shut out Will as it was what Will was about to say. The inevitable words. "OK, I have feelings. And I told her so."

"So let me guess. You told her, and she handed them right back to you."

"Right back at me on a silver platter."

"Ouch," Will said sympathetically.

"Ouch is right. But it was stupid. I knew she

didn't want to hear, well, anything like that. If there's one thing that's obvious about Summer, it's that she wants to stay separated. Works hard at it. Then here I go, blundering my way in…" He shook his head hard. "In a word, stupid."

"It's never stupid telling someone how you feel about them, even if your words only fall onto that silver platter. I'm guessing that whatever Summer's dealing with has nothing to do with you or the way she feels about you. But we all get overwhelmed sometimes, Rick. Don't know what to do or where to turn."

"In other words, she doesn't trust me."

"Could be. But maybe it's herself she doesn't trust."

"Which is something I can't change, or help her change, if she won't let me in. So maybe I should drop back to my original premise, that I'm good right where I am. Alone. No reason to make a change."

Will shrugged. "But the good cowboys always get right back up on their horses once they've been thrown. They don't get burned, Rick. They get back in the saddle and ride again."

Arching a skeptical eyebrow, Rick pushed his

empty beer mug back across the counter to Will. "Do you know what a stinking cliché that sounds like?"

Will chuckled as he refilled Rick's mug. "Stinking cliché maybe, but true. And for as long as I've known you, you've always climbed right back up there. Every time Rafe beat you up or Jess berated you, even that night at the senior prom when your date dumped you for me. As I recall, you walked out of there with two other guys' dates, one on each arm."

"And *you* married my date." Smiling, Rick hoisted his mug to that. "So here's to the better man who won the prettiest girl in town."

"And here's to getting back up instead of staying down," Will said, clinking his own glass, full of iced tea, to Rick's beer.

"And you're happy?" Rick asked on a sudden, almost sullen note.

"I'm happy. But the thing is, Marcie and I define our own happiness. For us it's those stolen moments alone that we don't get very often, or hauling the kids to soccer or ballet lessons. I'm not sure it would seem like true happiness to someone else, but to us it's perfect. You can have it too, Rick, even though your first try was bad. And whether or not it turns out to be with Summer, who knows? Just don't underestimate yourself when you finally find the perfect one like I did. I mean, look who I had to compete with to get Marcie." He leaned across the bar and gave Rick a playful punch in the arm. "If I'd underestimated myself in that situation for one second, I wouldn't be where I am and what I am today."

Did he really underestimate himself, or were his choices just plain bad? That was the question that plagued Rick all the way home, and held his attention through his bedtime story with Chris, then long into the night after that, even when he climbed into his big, empty king-sized bed alone and rolled over to face nothing or no one. It didn't matter, whichever it was. Alone was alone, and since he'd met Summer, it was harder to endure. "Damn hard," he muttered, shoving himself out of bed, grabbing up his blanket and heading to the lumpy couch in the living room. At least there he wouldn't have so much emptiness fighting him, or that deep-down *sleeping-alone-in-a-bed-for-two* feeling. Worst rotten damned feeling he could remember.

CHAPTER NINE

"I UNDERSTAND." Rick looked at the blinking numbers in the dark, red digits emphasizing the ungodly hour of three-fifteen a.m. "I'll alert the people here who need to know, and by the time you get the first round evacuated, we'll be ready for them."

He listened for another twenty seconds as Hank Lawson, chief-of-staff at Jasper's hospital, rattled off concerns and instructions. The man was a mess. He was evacuating his entire hospital, sending one hundred and thirty-two patients elsewhere, trying to keep a critical few alive during the transport as well as dispersing patients with new injuries who were presently banging on his front doors, looking for refuge. "So tell me what else we can do to help you," Rick said, once he could get a word squeezed in. "Do you need another medical team over there in Jasper? I can get one together for you, have them there within the hour."

"No," Hank said, sounding winded. "We've got the National Guard on its way to get the area evacuated, and the governor's sending in hazardous materials experts. In an hour there won't be anybody left here to treat…I hope. So the best thing you can do is take in as many of my patients as you can, then squeeze in a few more. Because all hell is breaking loose here, and I'm sending a lot of it your way. Now, reasonably, what can you handle?"

Rick did a quick mental assessment of what they could do without pushing their own resources to the limit. "OK, I can take seven or eight high-priority or critical cases, maybe another four or five lower priority serious cases. I'm good for about thirty routine cases, and if people don't mind bunching up, my ER can be good to go for at least twenty right off the bat, with at least that many more who can wait awhile. All ages, by the way. Oh, and, Hank, if the worst comes to the worst, just bring on what you have to, as long as you can send me some of your staff. We'll line the halls until we run out of hall space, if that's what we have to do."

Sure, there was rivalry between hospitals. Jasper was always the top regional facility, and that was the spot Rick wanted to claim and, hopefully, *would* claim once his expansion was completed. When there was an emergency, though, none of that mattered. "And, Hank, I'm giving you a direct order as your personal physician. Get the hell out of there. Right now! With your asthma, your lungs won't take the exposure, and I don't have time to mess with your stubbornness." Hank Lawson's condition worried him, considering how one of the most dangerous risks in a chlorine gas spill was lung injury. "You can come over here and see how a *real* hospital works."

"Appreciate the concern, Rick. I think I'll take you up on it so I can show your staff the value of maturity over youth in medical practice."

Hank was sixty-four. Vibrant. A real fighter for his staff and his patients. He'd also been Rick's doctor back in the days when the only doctor available in Lilly Lake had been Lawrence Corbett. All those years ago Rick hadn't understood why his mother dragged him all the way over to Jasper rather than seeking medical treatment from, well…as it turned out, his father. Now he knew, he was grateful she'd done that as Hank was as kind as Lawrence had been cruel. It had come as a surprise, in later years, when Rick was establishing himself in the Lilly Lake medical community, that Hank confided how much he'd despised Lawrence Corbett, as a man as well as a doctor. Wouldn't he be shocked now to know Lawrence was Rick's father? "One hour, Hank. I want to see you here in one hour, or I'll be sending out the troops to come get you."

Another glance at the red digital numbers on his clock didn't change a thing except the fact that time was ticking away and he had a hell of a lot ahead of him. First call…his brothers. Funny, how the word *brothers* came to mind so easily now. After that Summer. Then the rest of his key personnel. Calls he made as he was rousing Chris from a deep sleep. "Got an emergency at the hospital, sport," he said, scooping the boy out of bed and carrying him to his car. "Edie Corbett—" the aunt Chris didn't know he had "—is going to take care of you tonight and tomorrow."

"With Molly?" he mumbled in his drowsy state.

"With Molly." The cousin he didn't know he had. All the way over to Gracie House, it tweaked Rick's conscience. Chris *did* have a right to know who these people were to him, didn't he? Here he was, heading off to coordinate what was going to be the largest emergency he'd ever managed, thinking about his own mess rather than the disaster over in Jasper. A railroad car had derailed, leaking chlorine gas. There would be serious injuries, possibly fatalities. Hank Lawson, his dear friend, would succumb if he didn't get out of there. Rick's own staff was mobilizing now, his hospital was on the verge of an overload. And the simple thing, telling his family the truth, seemed as overwhelming as everything else going on. Except the people now involved in Jasper's disaster hadn't chosen their situation. But he'd chosen his, and tonight it wasn't sitting well with him. That train came through Lilly Lake and could have just as easily derailed here and, God forbid, lives close to him could have changed for ever.

Well, he wasn't going to think about all the possibilities in that scenario, except the one about where Chris would go if something ever happened to him. Actually, there was nothing to think about. He would go to family, of course. Rafe, or Jess. And they would raise him well. Rick knew that, trusted it. "My brothers," he murmured, now finally realizing what he had to do as he turned down the road to Gracie House and saw the progression of cars headed in the opposite direction, towards Lilly Lake Hospital. Here, he'd been hanging onto all these little bits of resentment, yet these were the men with whom he'd trust his son's life, and it was time to tell then the truth. Even so, the lingering fragments of bad feelings frustrated him and he wanted to shake them. Wanted to get them out of this head. How, though? That was the question, as well as the problem. How could he get rid of the past once, and for all, especially now that it affected Chris so deeply?

Was Summer going through the same thing, trying to rid herself of something from her past, something worse than a divorce? He wondered about that because something was clearly *off* in her life. Something she didn't trust him to help her with. Something big, something that kept her scared, kept her running. Yet who was he to help her when he hadn't helped himself? And that was the thing. All she'd seen from him was how he refused to help himself. Knew he wouldn't take that one small step that could change his life. So why *would* she think he could help her? He wanted to. Wanted to prove himself to her because, well…he'd told her he loved her, and he did. But telling was one thing. Now he had to prove it to her. And pretty damned fast because if he didn't he'd lose. This time around, he didn't want to. No. This time he *refused* to.

So, what was he going to do? No time to think about it now, not with his hospital on the verge of a crisis. Still, as he sped through the early morning, that's all he could think about. What the hell was he going to do to keep Summer here?

It was frustrating all the way around and Rick took out those frustrations on his steering-wheel, pounding it twice, while Chris snoozed quietly on the back seat, all strapped in with his favorite blanket and superhero action figure. Rick envied him the simplicity. Wished he could have a little of that himself.

"I'm good on triage, unless you want me somewhere else. But I'm not an emergency nurse, Rick. Haven't ever worked triage but I'm willing to do whatever I have to," Summer said. She was shoving every extra cart and piece of medical equipment aside in preparation for the patients who would start coming through the emergency doors any minute.

"Julie and Jess have the ER covered, we've got our doctors taking care of every other medical service and, as far as I know, we've got another dozen doctors and twice that many nurses coming in from Jasper. I've got your pediatrics ward staffed with several of our nurses, so you don't have to worry about that. And Rafe is in charge of getting the cafeteria and every other inch of available space he can find ready to take the non-critical patient overload. So I'd rather have someone I know on triage, and since you were in critical care before you came here, that's good enough for me. Also, I'm going to work the first wave of patients with you, so I can get a fix on what we're dealing with. In the meantime, I want to do a two-minute in-service for everybody in Admitting and Emergency, to make sure they're familiar with the symptoms of chlorine gas poisoning."

Time was running out. Dozens of patients were almost on their doorstep, and everyone employed by Lilly Lake Hospital, as well as half the town residents who'd come in to volunteer, were hustling to get everything ready. After the announcement of the in-service, inside a minute over fifty workers were huddled around the admitting desk, awaiting Rick's instructions.

"OK, everybody. Thanks for responding so fast. This is going to be a long one, lots of hard hours ahead of us. So I'm going to give you a quick crash course on chlorine gas poisoning, so you'll know what you're seeing in case you spot something else going on other than chlorine symptoms. Keep in mind we will probably have other injuries and illnesses to deal with that aren't related to chlorine gas."

Off to the side, Summer was watching Rick, not taking her eyes off him. He was in his element, leading the way he was. It suited him, but more than that he was a natural at it. He didn't have to think…he just knew. And she knew, too, that she loved him. Hadn't intended that to happen, but it had been growing, probably since the first day she'd met him. She'd known then, at first glance, that Rick Navarro was going to be trouble. Had known it the instant their eyes had met. He'd gazed, she'd glanced away then taken another shy peek, only to find him still gazing. Well, nothing about that had changed. He was still trouble, only now she had much deeper feelings, and ever deeper regrets that she could never act on those feelings.

Funny, how he'd said that he'd felt something for her at first sight, too. She wondered if, in a fairy-tale world, something like that could ever work out. Or was it doomed from the start? Too much too soon? Heart ruling head?

"So listen fast, because I don't have time to go over this again. I've prepared a list of primary and secondary symptoms to be watching for." He pointed to the stack of papers on the desk. "Everybody take one, keep it with you for reference. And be on the lookout for something that's exacerbating, or brought on by, another medical condition. You know, heart condition, asthma, emphysema. If you suspect that in your patient, get him or her to any of the designated critical care or emergency areas. Don't wait for a second opinion. Just do it." He took a deep breath. "Questions?"

"How far do we go with treatment at this stage?" Summer asked.

"Generally, oxygen, electrocardiogram, chest X-ray if you suspect something other than a mild presentation or you feel the symptoms warrant it. And if the symptoms are too severe, intubation and ventilator. It's going to be a judgment call in a good many of the cases, so go with your gut." He spent another minute going over various on-the-spot treatments then sent everybody to the stations with their symptom lists, except Summer, whom he pulled into an alcove. "Look, you're right. I've got to tell Rafe and Jess we're brothers. It really hit home for me when I was thinking about Chris, and who would raise him if something happened to me. I do trust either one of them to do that, and as soon as we get through this mess, that's the first thing I'm going to do."

Her eyes widened. "It's the right thing, Rick. I know it's not going to be easy for you, but you'll feel better about everything once you've told them."

"Well, then, let me warn you that the second thing I'm going to do is fight to keep you here. I don't know what it's going to take, Summer. Don't know what you need, but I'm not giving up."

She smiled, but didn't respond. Instead, she stroked his cheek with her hand and simply stared into his eyes. And the look in her eyes…it was so sad. A sadness he wanted to understand. And to fix. "Anyway, before we get all involved here, I wanted to thank you for…for being brutally honest with me. I needed it." With that, he brushed a tender kiss to her lips, then backed away, smiling. "Now, duty calls. But, Summer, it's not over."

Summer raised her hand to her lips, where it remained as she watched him hurry down the hall to greet the first wave of patients coming through the door. Then she drew in a deep breath, squared her shoulders, and joined Rick at the door.

"Take him to the cafeteria," Summer instructed, writing up a brief tag describing her patient's symptoms. Twenty-two in the door already, and it had only just begun.

"Got respiratory distress over here," one of the paramedics called. "Bilateral wheezing, coughing, cyanotic…"

The man was already wearing an oxygen mask, and he wasn't pinking up the way she would have wanted. Also, his wheezing could be heard audibly. No stethoscope needed. "Don't worry about me," he forced out, trying to wave her off. "I'll be fine."

She took a good look at him, and gasped, "Hank?" Dr Hank Lawson had been Grace's physician.

"Nice seeing you again, Summer," he said, forcing the words out through his wheezes.

"Nice seeing you, too, but not like this." A quick assessment of his pulse proved it to be thready and rapid. And his wheezing was increasing, too fast. "OK, I'm not going to hedge here because you know more about this than I do. First, don't try to talk. Just nod your head. Do you have a pre-existing respiratory condition?"

He nodded.

"Emphysema?"

This time he indicated no.

"Asthma, then?"

His indication was in the affirmative, and she immediately went through her options for a quick treatment, something to sustain him until they could give me more intensive care. "Can you take albuterol...nebulized?"

"With lidocaine," he whispered. "Good cough suppressant."

She took a fast listen to his chest, knew the situation was getting dire. This man was on the verge of total respiratory collapse and she had serious concern that a bronchodilator with lidocaine would be enough. Which was why, when she stepped away from him for a moment and asked one of the aids to get a nebulizer then sent an order to the pharmacy for the medication, she also gave Rick a call. "He's cyanotic," she told him. "Pulse fast and thready, blood pressure high, he's beginning to cough, and his breath signs are decreasing. I've got a nebulizer order and albuterol with a one percent solution of lidocaine, but I think we need to get ready for a ventilator."

"I'll be there in less than a minute," Rick said. "And, Summer, good call. I told him to get out of that damned gas immediately, but he's one stubborn old doctor. Patients come first, and I have an idea he was the last one out the hospital door."

The way Rick would be. She understood that.

"So, Hank, I think your physician might have some words for you," Summer said as she dispensed the medication into the nebulizer, a device that would aerosolize the medicine for Hank to breath in.

"He's stubborn," Hank said.

"And you're not?" She arched amused eyebrows. "Seems to me you and Rick have that in common."

"That's where I learned it," Rick said, stepping up to the stretcher and immediately putting his stethoscope to the man's chest. "Hank was the best teacher anybody could have when it comes to stubbornness…" Straightening, he tucked his stethoscope back into his pocket and gave Summer a barely perceptible nod.

"I know that look," Hank said. "Used it once or twice myself."

"And I know that Nurse Adair told you not to talk," Rick retorted, laying a reassuring hand on Hank's shoulder. "So you'd better do what she says. Anyway, you've got some edema building up in your lungs, especially the left one, and we're going to have to make sure it doesn't lead to something else. In the meantime, I'm not going to do a bronchoscopy yet, especially while you're in bronchospasm, but I am going to have X-ray get some shots of your chest so we'll know exactly what we're dealing with. I'm also going to order up steroids to see if that will get rid of some of this problem, then we'll go from there. You know what can happen, Hank. You keep going the wrong way and I may have to intubate and put you on a ventilator, and my concern with that is weaning you off since you're a chronic-lunger. It's not always easy, which is why I'm going to be very conservative in treating you. I'm also going to order a blood gas and an EKG, standard tests for your condition, and they should tell me a lot more before I make any decisions other than basic treatment. Oh, and just to keep you from getting up and trying to treat patients, I've got a bed waiting for you in ICU, right next to the nurses' station so they can keep an eye on you."

Hank waved Rick off with the flick of a wrist, then smiled and winked at Summer. Then he turned his attention back to Rick. "You're the doctor," he said, his voice so frail now it barely squeaked out. Then he shut his eyes, inhaled deeply, and concentrated on breathing in all the medicine being nebulized.

"How bad is his asthma?" Summer asked, once the X-ray technician rolled the portable X-ray machine into place.

"He should probably retire from the hospital, but he won't. So someday it will probably kill him." He glanced fondly at the man. "But not today. Look, I know you're busy here…everybody's going crazy. But I'd appreciate it if you…"

She squeezed his arm. "Just give me a minute to go and ask Julie if she can handle triage while I'm gone, then I won't leave his side until he's in ICU."

"I know most people would say they couldn't do this without you, but I want you to know that I don't want to do this without you, Summer. I was serious when I told you it wasn't over. Because it's not. I don't know what's going on in your life that you can't trust me with, but I'm going to find out, then I'm going to deal with it, help you through it."

"You can't always get what you want, Rick."

"That's what you think."

"That's what I know," she whispered to herself once he was out of earshot. Her knight in shining armor had finally arrived. But too late. Because she not only couldn't get what she wanted, she couldn't get what she needed. In the end, that's the way it always worked out. She knew that but yet there was still that hidden place inside her where she wanted it to work out so badly she ached.

"Third wave?' Summer slumped against the wall, and raised one foot as if that would help the general fatigue spreading through her body after seven hours on duty and passing more than one hundred patients through her doors. "We have a third wave of patients coming in? I thought that last bunch was it for us, except for some tricklers."

"They're not critical," Rick explained, slumping alongside her. "Most of them have been working the gas leak, a couple of them are holdouts who wouldn't evacuate until it became critical."

"Where are we going to put them? Every available inch of space is already taken up."

Rick chuckled. "I guess this is where one of us has to become creative, isn't it?"

"Assuming that's you, since my mind is too numb to think. So, how many more should we expect? Any idea?"

"They told me not more than ten or fifteen, so that probably means twenty or twenty-five."

"So somewhere between ten and twenty-five people with nowhere to go." Stretching, twisting her back from side to side then rolling her shoulders to relieve her sore muscles, she let out a weary groan. "Guess I'll have to make everybody get even friendlier and squeeze closer together." Circling her neck, she reached up to rub it, but Rick beat her to it, and his hands were heaven. Everything she could have hoped for, and more.

"Tell me where it hurts."

"Anywhere you care to massage." Groaning involuntarily as his fingers kneaded that sensitive spot where her neck connected to her shoulders, she practically melted back against him but, after enjoying his fingers for a few moments, forced herself to remember where they were and what they were doing. "Do you moonlight as a massage therapist?" she practically purred, trying to summon up the will to step away.

"You're my first."

"Your first? Then you're a—"

"Massage virgin," he interrupted. "Yes. But like everything else, if I'm allowed to practice, I'll get better."

Sighing the sigh of a satiated woman, she said, "Trust me, your hands are perfect." Hands she dearly wanted to massage someplace other than her neck. A thought that, when it hit her, was the one that caused her to move away. What in the world was she doing? One little massage…

shoulders only…and she wanted more. Then more would lead to other wants, other needs and, well… It didn't matter. There was safety in distance, and several quick steps to the other side of the hall would take care of that. Physically, anyway. Emotionally, she was drained, and it had nothing to do with the hospital's emergency. "Anyway, as much as I appreciate the massage, I've got patients on the way in, and I guess it's time to figure out what I'm supposed to do with them."

"Can we talk later?"

"What's there to say, Rick?"

"I don't know. By then, maybe I will."

"We'll see. But no promises, OK?" No promises because nothing had changed. She wouldn't…couldn't…tell him the truth. Her lie to live, his to deal with, she supposed.

"No promises," he agreed. Yet the look on his face was that of a man who wanted promises.

"Well, except for the fact that Dietary's scrambling for food, we've got several of our suppliers on the way with emergency provisions, there's no more room for anybody unless we want to start stacking patients on top of each other, and our medical staff is stretched to its limits and exhausted, I think we're in pretty good shape." Rick dropped down on the couch in the doctors' lounge, alongside Rafe and across from Jess. "No fatalities, two extreme criticals, five high-priority criticals, six moderate-to low-priority criticals, and I don't remember how many general admittances we've had come in. Could I just tell you a whole bunch, and get those numbers to you later?"

Rafe chuckled. "Don't worry about it. As they say, it's quality, not quantity, that counts."

"Well, I'm not sure how much quality you can give them when you can't even squeeze yourself down the halls, but I'm doing my best."

Jess pulled the chair next to him over, leaned back, propped his feet up on it. "Actually, you're doing one hell of a job for short notice, a facility under reconstruction, and limited resources."

Rafe chuckled. "Tell that to the guy we've got stashed in the broom closet. He's pretty grumpy about the whole thing."

Rafe moaned. "Really? We have a patient in the broom closet?"

"No. The chief of staff. That's where I ended up when we started taking over the admin offices for patient care. So my choice was the closet or the parking lot." Rick grinned. "Just me and the mops. Good news is, I think we've generated some good publicity out of this."

"Yeah. I saw the news crew come though a few hours ago," Jess said. "I didn't have time to talk to them…"

"But they were filming in the background, weren't they?" Rick asked. "I told them they weren't allowed to get any specific patient footage."

"They were being good, not getting in the way. It's going to be helpful, though, letting the whole area see what we're going through. Maybe it will bring in some donations."

"Ah, yes…it's always a fiscal matter, isn't it?" Rafe quipped. He looked point-blank at Rick. "One of the joys of hospital ownership, if you'd care to join Jess and me."

Instead of responding to Rafe, Rick picked up the television's remote control, turned on the set then clicked through the channels until he came to the news, which was broadcasting a live remote from Jasper. "Looks like things are clearing up, finally," he commented. "Will Brassard told me they probably wouldn't let anybody go back home for several days, to be on the safe side."

"We're going over with a crew tomorrow morning to relieve whoever's working there," Jess said. "Which means it's time for me to go off duty as a doctor, head on home and get a few hours' sleep before I'm on duty as a fireman." He pushed himself out of his chair and headed for the door. "Coming with me, big brother? I'll bet your wife will be glad to get you home."

"Not any gladder than *I'll* be to get home. Give me a ride? I'm too tired to drive."

Jess laughed. "I was just about to ask you the same thing."

As Rafe and Jess dragged themselves out the door, Rick thought about their relationship, and how good it was. In a way, he envied that. Even if he entered the family mix now, he'd never have that with them. Of course, Rafe and Jess had been estranged for years and were only now getting back together. But would they ever be able to accept him as one of them…as their brother? Or would old feelings and new resentments pop up?

Truth was, he didn't know and, right now he was too tired to worry about it. He was on break for two hours, going to take a nap before he went back to work. So he kicked off his shoes, stretched out his legs on the couch, and propped a pillow behind his head, fully intent on dozing off to the drone of the reporter. *"Lilly Lake Hospital, one of the regional hospitals vested with the responsibility of taking in those evacuated from Jasper..."*

The words drifted though Rick's brain as he was halfway to slumber, but he opened his eyes to look at the screen and saw Summer there. She was moving from one patient to another, taking pulses, making assessments. Beautiful image to drift off to sleep with. *Rather be drifting off with Summer*, he thought.

"No," she choked, staring up at the TV screen. "They didn't..." She hadn't even seen the news cameras. Lord knew, she wouldn't have let them film her if she had. "Don't panic," she told herself, looking frantically for the exit. She needed air. Needed space. Needed to get out of there. "This is local…he wouldn't have seen it."

But didn't local news footage sometimes make it through to national feeds? An entire town evacuated because of chlorine gas was big news. The odds of that one shot with her in triage… and it wasn't even that close up, was it? Would Cameron see it and recognize her?

"Oh, my God," she whispered. This couldn't be happening. Not again. Not now! She wasn't ready. But she had to be. Had to get Alyssa, had to pack a few things. Had to go…she just didn't know where.

CHAPTER TEN

"Rɪᴄᴋ, there's a gentleman in the hall who asked to see the chief-of-staff," Julie Corbett said. "I'm not sure what he wants, but he's pretty…let's just call it insistent. He said he hired a private jet and flew here, and he doesn't have time to wait."

"And I don't have time to meet with anybody," Rick said, keeping his voice purposely low. "Not until after I get through with my rounds." He looked down at Hank Lawson, who was snoozing peacefully and breathing better, much to his relief. "Tell him I'll be taking a break in about three hours, if I'm lucky, and I'll meet with him then, if he wants to wait."

"I don't have three hours to wait," the man said, marching into the ICU. He was an imposing force with a well-practiced scowl on his face. "And what I require of you will take very little time."

Rick bristled instantly. "I'm sorry, but you

can't be in here. Leave now, or I'll call Security."
He gave a discreet nod to Julie, who backed out
to do just that.

"Like I said, Doctor, this will only take a minute."

"In case you haven't noticed, we're busy right
now. I don't *have* a minute to give you and the
longer you stand and argue with me, the more
I'll be disinclined to have a minute for you any
time later. So, please, leave my intensive care
unit."

"First, let me explain myself. My name is
Cameron Carson. *Judge* Cameron Carson. So
you'll know, I sit on the bench of the Supreme
Court of the State of California, and I do have
judicial *friends* in New York who will assist me,
if that becomes necessary."

The man was threatening him with friends
in power? Now Rick was angry, not just about
Judge Carson's intrusion but about how much
he was like Lawrence Corbett who had always
been quick to pull an influential friend out of
his hip pocket when he'd needed one. No way in
hell the judge was going to get his minute now.
"And so *you'll* know, you're about to be escorted

out to the parking lot." He gave the nod to the two security guards Julie had alerted, and they stepped in, each one taking Cameron Carson by an armpit, attempting to drag him out.

But he shrugged them off. "You're harboring my wife here, as well as my daughter."

That piqued Rick's interest a little. "Harboring? As patients?"

"No, not as patients. I believe my wife is a member of your staff, Doctor. Her name is Wendy Carson. She's a registered nurse."

Not a name he recognized. "Sorry," Rick said without hesitation. "She doesn't work here. Maybe in one of the other regional hospitals…"

"If that's your position, you're lying because I saw her on a news report and she was identified not by name but as a nurse at Lilly Lake Hospital. So if you insist on denying me access to her, and especially to my daughter…let's just say this is going to get very ugly for you and your little hospital."

Smug bastard, Rick thought. If Wendy Carson *was* hiding from her husband, he couldn't blame her. The man was a bully, and if Mrs. Carson was trying to get away from him, trying to keep herself hidden…

A cold chill suddenly shot up Rick's spine as he thought about the news report broadcast earlier. The only nurse he'd seen featured prominently in that minute segment had been… "Take him out!" Rick demanded. "Now! Show him to the parking lot, and if he resists, call the police and have the judge arrested for trespassing."

Cameron Carson spun around and stormed into the hallway of his own volition, but once there he stood at the window and glared back in at Rick for a moment before the guards escorted him out.

"Any idea what this is about?" Julie asked.

Rick hesitated for a second, then shrugged. "Not sure. But…" That cold chill came back, even colder this time, and he knew it wasn't going away any time soon. Not until he knew…

"Look, I've got to run a quick errand out of the hospital. Everything is settled down enough for me to leave, so there shouldn't be any problems. And we've had a whole new medical staff come in from Jasper, *rested*, so we're covered. But if you need me…" He held up his cellphone.

"Do you need help, Rick?"

"With what?"

Julie shrugged. "I don't know, but that look on your face… I have this feeling…"

"No. I'm fine. I just want to run by Rafe and Edie's and check in on Chris for a couple minutes, then I need to…" Find Summer? Then what? Ask her how just much she'd been lying to him all along? "Regroup. So, no, I don't need any help. But, thanks."

"If Cameron Carson is still in the parking lot," Julie yelled down the hall after him, "be careful, Rick. I don't trust the man."

Neither did he. And he didn't want to think about why.

"OK, sweetheart, we're playing a game. We're going to see how fast we can put everything from your closet into the back seat of Mommy's car."

"Don't want to!" Alyssa complained, folding stubborn little arms across her chest. "Johnny Redmond said I could go ride a pony with him."

"There will be lots of ponies to ride later on," Summer said, scooping up an armload of her own clothes and cramming them into a suitcase. "After we play the game." She hated lying to her daughter, but this was what Cameron was forcing her to do. She didn't have another choice. "And we'll stop for ice cream with sprinkles later on."

"Don't want ice cream. Want to ride the pony." Alyssa stuck out her pouty lower lip, then sat down on the living room carpet, cross-legged. "I don't like your game, Mommy."

Summer exhaled an exasperated breath. It wasn't fair. None of this was. "Fine, you stay where you are while I pack…er, play the car game." She didn't have time to argue with her daughter. A quick call to the television station had put her into even more of a panic. The segment with herself in it had been sent out nationally. And the broadcast she'd seen had been the third time it had aired…the first time had been four hours before. Four hours!

This was everything she'd dreaded, and everything she'd avoided preparing for. But now that it was descending on her, she really didn't care what they left behind. None of it mattered. They needed a few clothes, some of Alyssa's toys and favorite blankets. Clancy was in the cat carrier, marginally miffed about the inconvenience but being placated with food. And she had to bring her photos. That's all they were taking this time as it wasn't like she was packing for a casual move to a new house. She was running for her life due to the one thing she'd totally refused to think about, the last words she'd ever heard from Cameron… *You know what I can, and will, do.*

Yes, she did. That's why she was shoving the last armload of clothes in the back of the car. Next time in her front door would be her last. She'd grab her daughter and never look back.

"Alyssa, honey…it's time to take a ride," she called on her way back in, heading to the kitchen to grab snacks and drinks so they wouldn't have to stop for a while. "Go have one last look at your bedroom and see if there's anything else you want to take along for the game, then go to the bathroom…"

She stashed bottled water, crackers, cookies, loose fruit, peanut butter and a loaf of bread into the bag, then went to check on Alyssa. "Alyssa," she called again, fighting to keep the mounting panic out of her voice. "Did you hear me, sweetheart?"

No answer, so she poked her head into Alyssa's room, only to find it empty. She padded down the hall to the bathroom, but the door was open. No Alyssa in there. Or in Summer's bedroom, or the den, or the sunroom. "Alyssa!" she called, over and over, each time louder until finally, she was screaming. "Alyssa, please!"

Panic crushed down on her, sucking out her breath, bringing her to her knees. Her daughter… Had Cameron…? "No!" she screamed, bolting up and running hard to the front door, where she ran straight into Rick, who had Alyssa in his arms.

"She said she was going for a pony ride," he said. "Apparently, Johnny promised, and you wouldn't let her. Or something like that."

Without a word, Summer grabbed her daughter away from him and ran to her car.

"What the hell is happening?" Rick yelled, spinning around, taking in the sheer panic that was driving her to do whatever it was she was doing then going after her. By the time he reached the door, she was already inside, Alyssa was strapped in her seat, the car door locked, and Summer was trying to start the engine. No way she was going to get back out, or even roll down the window and tell him what was happening, so he sprinted to the front of the car, placed his hands palms down on the hood, and simply stood there.

"Get out of my way!" she screamed at him. "Rick, please…"

"Not until you tell me what this is about."

"I'm leaving. I can't be here any more. Please, just let me go."

"Mommy, you promised ice cream," Alyssa whimpered

"I've got to go…now, Rick! Don't you understand? I've got to get away from this place right now."

"Mommy…" Alyssa whined.

"Is it about Judge Cameron Carson, Summer? Tell me what it is. We can work it out. Whatever it is, we can work it out together."

"He's here?"

Rick nodded. "He came to the hospital, and—"

"I can't do this. We can't. Not any more. I have to…"

"Mommy…" Alyssa whined yet again.

Summer whipped around, glared at her daughter in the back seat. "Alyssa, not now!" she yelled. "Not now!" Then, realizing that she'd yelled at her daughter, she turned back around and dropped her head into her steering wheel, covered her head with her arms and let the tears flow. She couldn't keep on living like this any more. It was too tough. It was affecting her daughter. But what was her alternative? She couldn't stay, yet she couldn't go.

To her left, Rick tapped on the window. "Let me in," he said. "Whatever this is, whatever you're afraid of, you can't go through it alone."

Much to his relief, she hit the power lock and within a second he was sitting in the passenger's seat, holding Summer in his arms while she sobbed. "I yelled at her, Rick. I…I didn't mean to, but…"

"I know you did," he said, gently rocking Summer as he looked over the seat at Alyssa, whose attention was totally caught up in a toy pony, a purple one with a long, yellow tail. "And she's fine, Summer."

"But you don't understand," Summer sniffled, her head still tucked into his chest.

"Not unless you tell me. But I think I might know the beginning of the story..."

Eyes wet, tears streaming down her cheeks, she finally looked up at him. Feeling safe. This was where she felt safe! "I don't understand."

"The beginning. Where you're Mrs. Wendy Carson, and your husband is abusing you, so you ran away. That *is* the beginning, isn't it?"

She pushed herself away from Rick, away from the safety of his arms, and sat straight up. "How long have you known?" she asked, swiping back tears with the sleeve of her shirt.

"About thirty minutes. After I met him, I figured it out. He reminds me of Lawrence Corbett, by the way."

"I can't believe he's really here. So fast. I mean, I knew if he saw the news broadcast he'd come looking. But I thought we had more time."

"He hired a private jet to get him here, Summer. The man's in a hurry."

"Of course he is. And Cameron has the money and power to do whatever he wants."

"So he let me know."

Summer drew in a deep breath. "I've been running a long time. Tried to get away from him before, and he dragged me back, then told me I'd never see…" She didn't say the words, but the way she looked over the seat at her daughter said everything. "Even now, sometimes when I go to sleep, I have this nightmare where he's chasing me and I can't get away from him. I'll wake up in a sweat, gasping for breath…my life, Rick. That's been my life and for so long there was nothing I could do because he always…always found me or threatened me. Anyway, there's this underground network for abused wives, ex-wives and women who need to get their children away from an abusive father. The law doesn't always protect us, but the volunteers who run the network help get us away, hide us, give us new identities and set us up in new lives. That's where I met Grace. She was an angel to the women who needed her, and I needed her more than she needed a nurse. So here we were, two people who needed each other, and she took me in."

"I'm not surprised she was involved."

"She always felt guilty she couldn't get Rafe and Jess away, so this was how she made up for it. What she couldn't do in her own family what she did for others in the same situation. I'm in Lilly Lake because Grace was atoning for Rafe and Jess's abuse. For your mother's, too, I think. Anyway, I, um… You don't need to get involved in this, Rick. I'm going to leave. You can tell Cameron…tell him anything you want. I don't even want to put you into the position of lying to him, so you can tell him I ran away… again. That's all you have to know, and he won't be able to hurt you with it. Now, please, get out of my car."

"And if I don't?"

She squared herself in the seat, and started the engine. "Then you go with me. And when we stop at a motel for the night and you go in to take a shower, or go to sleep, or the next time we stop for gas and you run into the gas station for a soda, I'll run away from you, too. I'm good at it."

"Tell me that's how you want to spend the rest of your life, Summer? *Tell me.* Look me straight in the eyes, say the words and convince me that running away is what you want to do. And I can read your eyes, Summer. Read the lies there, as well as the truth. So tell me, is this what you want?"

"But you *know* you can't always get what you want, Rick," she said, avoiding the eye contact he wanted.

He reached over, gave her hand a gentle squeeze. "But if you try sometimes…"

Summer shook her head, swatted back a tear. "I'm not going to get what I need. It's way past time for that, after what I did. Maybe I should have stayed and fought, but the battle against his power…I didn't have time to wage it because I was afraid for Alyssa. So I made my choices and there's no going back."

"He…" Rick glanced back at Alyssa, who was absorbed playing with her pony, then back at Summer. He mouthed the word *abused*. "…you, didn't he?"

She nodded, and motioned him out of the car for the rest of it.

"But that's what *he* did," Rick said, on his way around to the passenger side, where Summer was leaning against the driver's door. "Not you, not your choice. You were only protecting yourself and your child. Did he ever hurt her?"

"He came close. Raised his fist...that's the day I took her and ran. The day I knew I had to do whatever I had to in order to protect her. And the thing is, people wonder why we...and I mean *all* the women who find themselves in my position...they wonder why we stay. They think we're weak, or we don't have other choices, or we're not smart enough to do better... Everybody has an opinion, but they don't know. Even you had an opinion, Rick, and you told me *yourself* that you wondered why your mother stayed with your father. You were angry when you first started to suspect what he was doing. You were angry because she *allowed* it to happen. And you were disappointed with her. Your relationship changed because of what *you* thought.

"Well, I lived with that, tried everything I could do, but Cameron had leverage..." She glanced back in at her daughter. "He would have used her, used the one person I love more than my own life and every time...*every time* I tried to get away, tried to fight him, he fought me harder, threatened me, hurt me even more than he had before. Maybe that's what your father did to your mother, Rick. Had you ever thought of that? She was an immigrant, illegal at first… Could he have threatened her with *you*? Was that what kept her with him until you were old enough to leave? Because the one thing I know more than anything else is that I have done, and will do, whatever it takes to protect my daughter from her father."

"Oh, my God," Rick whispered, slumping next to Summer on the door. "I never…never thought about it like that."

"Your mother loved you, Rick. And she lived in a difficult world, trying to take care of you the best she knew how. I know that world. It's cruel. It hurts the people you love the most. Which is why I'm asking you to get out of my car now, before Cameron finds us. *And he will*."

"You can win this, Summer. You don't have to deal with him alone any more."

"See, that's the thing. I have to deal with it alone, because I don't have full custody of my daughter. I was fighting for it, but the judge on the case…he was a friend of Cameron's and believed Cameron when he said I wasn't stable. It was a battle I couldn't win."

"But didn't you have medical records to prove the abuse?"

"Of stupid accidents. That's what I always told them because my dutiful husband was the one who took me to the hospital. He never left my side when I was treated. So I fell down. Or I walked into a door. Those are my medical records, not the ones where I say he hit me, he kicked me, he knocked me down a flight of stairs. Those don't exist."

"Why?"

"Because I had something in my life more important than me, and Cameron told me if I ever so much as uttered the word 'abuse' he'd take her away and I'd never see her again. That's when I realized just what I'd do to protect someone I loved. I had to choose what I loved most."

"So you ran away."

She nodded. "I had to. I think, in time, he probably would have killed me. I might have broken my neck when I *tripped* and fell down a flight of stairs or hit my head on the edge of a table during one of my *clumsy* stages and sustained a fatal wound. Was it inevitable? I don't know. Was it possible? Absolutely. And all I could think of was that if I died, Cameron would raise Alyssa." She shook her head violently. "I couldn't let that happen."

"That son of a…" He choked off his words, fought for control. "Summer, I'm so sorry. You didn't deserve this. Nobody does and now I wish to God my mother had talked to me, told me something…*anything*…to make me understand. We could have had a different life. It's too late for that, but it's not too late for you…for us."

"It is, Rick. I could have done something different, but I was so scared. And the last time he hit me I snapped. It was brutal and Alyssa saw it. It was the first time she ever… Anyway, afterwards, he went to the golf course for the afternoon like nothing ever happened and I…I took her and we were three states away before I'd even realized what I was doing. I just drove. Couldn't think. Couldn't sleep or eat. *I just drove.* Which is what I have to do right now."

"But do you want to stay?" Rick asked. "If this mess could be fixed, and we could get Cameron out of your life for good, would you want to stay in Lilly Lake, and raise your daughter here?"

"More than anything in the world." Summer swallowed hard. "But how?"

"Start by trusting me."

"You're the only one I do trust. But it's going to take more than trust, and…I can't fight the fight any longer. I'm tired, Rick," she said, as the tears flooded down her face again. "But I can't let him win either."

"Mommy?" Alyssa called out to her.

Summer opened the car door. "What, sweetheart?"

"Are you sick, Mommy? Is Dr Rick going to fix you?"

"No, sweetheart, Mommy's not sick. She's just a little sad today because we're going on a new adventure and Dr Rick can't come with us right now."

"But can he come later?"

"I hope so. I really hope so."

"I love you," Rick whispered in her ear. "Everything I've said in the past about not wanting to get involved again, and all those things about my mother, that was the *idiot* Rick Navarro who existed before he knew how much he loved Summer Adair, before Summer Adair opened his eyes to the things he should have known, should have been more tolerant of. The much wiser Rick Navarro who exists now isn't that stupid any more, and he'll grab his son and run away with you, if that's what he has to do."

Smiling, Summer stroked his cheek. "You were the man I always wanted, Rick. There have been so many times when I've watched you, wishing you were Alyssa's dad…"

"You're going to be my new daddy?" Alyssa piped up cheerfully.

"No, sweetheart. Rick isn't going to be your new daddy. He still has to be Chris's daddy, and that takes up most of his time."

"OK," Alyssa said, quite unaffected, then turned her attention back to her toys.

"The innocence of youth," Summer said, trying to deflect the escalating emotion of the moment.

"Or the wisdom of it."

"We can't do this, Rick! Can't even think it." She lowered her voice even more. "He won't let me go. He'll always find me, and when he does, he'll hurt the people I love, the people who love me. That's never going to change because

Cameron's never going to change. He's a cruel man who needs people around him to be cruel to. So please leave. It's over. Everything between us is over. It has to be."

"What's between us, Summer? I love you. You know it, and I know it. But what about you? Do you have any feelings for me?"

"Does it matter?"

He nodded. "To me, it does. I have to know."

"And if I tell you, what will that do?"

"Make me move heaven and earth."

He deserved to hear the truth. It wouldn't change things, not for her. But Rick did deserve to know. "Yes, I love you. More than I knew any woman could ever love a man. And I never wanted to hurt you with any of this, Rick. Never wanted it to touch you, or even come close to you or Chris, which is why we never..."

"Never what, Summer?"

"Kissed, or anything else. Because if I ever did, I knew I couldn't leave you. And I have to...to protect you." A soft smile curved to her lips. "But if we'd ever, well, done *anything*, even dated casually, I would have loved that."

He arched speculative eyebrows. "Then you want me?"

"For months you're all I've wanted. Just the two of us…or the four of us." She sighed. "I wish we could have it, but how can we have a real life when we know that we might have to leave it behind at any moment?"

"I admire how much you want to protect the people you love, Summer. It makes me love you all the more. But you don't have to do this alone now. You're not alone now."

"You hate the lies, Rick, and that all I've been doing—lying to you almost from the moment we met. And your mother…you said the same thing about her, about how not knowing the truth hurt you. How she disappointed you. The thing is, I wanted to tell you, but I was so afraid. Then after a while it wasn't fear so much as knowing you'd be disappointed in me, too."

"I was wrong, but I'm learning, Summer. I'm a work in progress. Be patient with me, I have a way to go."

"And not telling you everything? That lie by omission doesn't make you want to walk away from me the way you did from your mother?"

He leaned across the seat and brushed a tender kiss to her lips. "It's what you believed you had to do. I understand that. And understanding that in you has made me understand what my mother did. Because of you, I'm going to be able to come to terms with a lot of things."

"We all make our choices, Rick. Maybe the choices would be better if we had someone we loved and trusted there to help us make them. Sometimes, though, we have to make them alone."

"Except you're not alone. I know that's hard for you to trust, but I'm a patient man, and I'll do whatever it takes, however long it takes, to make you believe it."

"I want to. With all my heart, I really want to. But, Cameron…"

Suddenly, Rick stepped away from the car. "If you trust me, Summer, *really trust me*, you'll go to Jess's cabin and stay there until you hear from me again. If this is what you truly want. And I think it is, Summer. That's the thing *I'm* going to trust." Then he headed off toward his car, and got in.

The last Summer saw of Rick was the cloud

of dust his car kicked up on the dirt road leading off the Gracie Estate.

No, this wasn't the way he'd planned it. Truth
was, he hadn't planned it at all, but there was
nothing else he could do. Not more putting off
anything. It was time, even though he sure as
hell didn't know how it was going to turn out.
"It's only a photocopy," he explained to the three
men sitting in front of him. "I've got the original
letter, if you want to have it verified. Summer
was the one who found it, and she was there
when I opened it…don't know if that has any
legal bearing or not."

Rafe looked up from the letter. "This is what
she found when she was looking for the baby
dress?"

"It was in a box on the shelf in what's now the
nursery."

"Well, I'd wondered what it was. Figured you'd
tell us when you were ready."

"I wanted to do it differently. Do it better. To
be honest, I was still wrestling with whether I
even wanted to tell you at all."

"You didn't want to tell them?" Henry Danforth

asked. He was the Corbett family attorney, and a trusted family friend.

"I went back and forth. Sometimes I did, sometimes I didn't."

"But as her nephew, you're entitled to one third of everything Grace owned. Surely, that should have motivated you."

"I'd say you'd also be entitled to a third of the old man's estate, too, but apart from the land, which we kept for Gracie Foundation, we donated the rest of it to…well, the Gracie Foundation." Jess smiled. "Rafe and I decided to let the old man do some good for a change."

"It's not about the inheritance," Rick said defensively. "It's about being a Corbett. My *Corbett* father bullied my mother, my *Corbett* brothers bullied me for years. So tell me, *who*, in their right mind, would want to be part of that?"

"Maybe you're right about that, but the one thing you didn't take into consideration was that Grace Corbett loved you," Rafe added. "It doesn't right all the wrongs, but it's one hell of a Corbett legacy, being related to that great lady." He chuckled. "And now you *officially* own part of the hospital. As far as I'm concerned, things are working out fine." He smacked Jess on the shoulder. "Didn't anticipate we'd get him this way, little brother, but we did it! Or should I say Aunt Grace did it."

"Well, I may have the hospital, but I may not be staying. I'm in love with Summer Adair—"

"Not surprised," Jess interrupted. "Rafe and I had a bet."

"Well, don't fork over any more yet. Because this is where it gets complicated. I'm sure you heard about that guy who walked right into the ICU earlier today and tried to cause trouble…"

It had been three hours now…three that seemed like ten. Alyssa was sleeping peacefully, without a care in the world, while Summer's stomach was turning to acid. "I should have gone," she whispered to a sparrow hopping its way along the outer ledge of the front picture window. "Flown away, the way you're getting ready to do." But she wanted a chance with Rick, and prayed he'd be able to give her that chance…give them all that chance, as a family. During her first hour she'd been confident he could make it happen. All hopes and jitters. That confidence had waned in the second hour, when her stomach had started to churn. Now, almost all the way through the third, she had her car keys in her hand, weighing her decision again.

Except she didn't want to go, and as much as the part of her that compelled her to run was nagging at her to get away from there as fast as she could, the part that was telling her this was home was pulling her back even harder. In her heart, *and her head*, Summer knew it was time to quit hurting, time to believe in the trust she had in Rick. Believe in Rick.

"Mommy, I want a drink of water," Alyssa cried from the bedroom.

Summer went to the kitchen, got a glass of water and took it to the bedroom, but when she got there…

"Hello, Wendy…or is it Summer now?" Cameron stood blocking the entrance to the bedroom just as bold as you please. "I'll admit, you're getting better at this. I'd have never taken you for a small-town girl, yet here you are."

The glass slipped from Summer's hand and shattered on the floor, sending shards of glass, ice cubes and water everywhere. "How'd you get in?" she choked, stepping backwards.

"Back door. Apparently, people around here don't think locks are so important. Oh, and so you don't have to ask the next question, I knew you were here because I asked around town. Showed your picture, asked if anybody had seen you. As it turned out, *everybody* was anxious to tell me about all about your life, and your little house on the….what is they call it? The Gracie Estate. But you weren't there when I went looking, so another fishing trip netted me information about this cabin. People here are friendly, very chatty. *Very* unassuming."

"You can't do this, Cameron. Not any more."

"Oh, but I can." He pulled a blue-backed legal form from the breast pocket of his custom-tailored blue suit. "And I will. This is sole custody of Alyssa, granted to me on the basis of… well, let me spare you the details. They were pretty ugly. And I think you always knew what I was going to tell them. Anyway, I've had this about a year now, which means, legally, you're a kidnapper." He grinned. "Let her go without a fight, Wendy, and we'll forget that part of it.

But take one step closer to me, or lift one hand to stop me from taking my daughter, and you're going to prison. That's the only deal you're getting here, except the one where I let you have *supervised* visitation rights, one hour a month. That makes me look like the better person, allowing my ex-wife, the one who ran away with our daughter, see her daughter."

"You're a bully," she said, fighting to keep her calm. "And an abuser."

"That from the lips of a woman who never reported an abuse?" He laughed. "Who's going to believe you, Wendy? Give me one name."

"We'll give you three," Rick Corbett said, stepping around the corner, followed by his brothers. "My name is Dr Rick Navarro, in case you didn't remember. And these are my brothers, Dr Rafe Corbett and Dr Jess Corbett."

Summer spun around to see them. Standing shoulder to shoulder, they were an impressive wall of men…led by the most impressive man she'd ever known. Rick took her breath away. In fact, all the Corbett brothers took her breath away, and she was so happy they'd come as brothers. No matter how this turned out, Rick had his family now. More than that, his family had Rick. "They're not going to let you do this, Cameron," she said, turning back to face him. "You may think you're formidable, but you haven't dealt with the Corbetts."

He smiled. "Actually, there's nothing they can do to stop me."

"That's where you're wrong," Rick stated, stepping up to Cameron, actually towering over him by a couple of inches and outsizing him by several inches of pure, hard muscle. He shoved a paper in Cameron's chest. "This is where you're officially stopped."

Cameron took a quick glance, then laughed. "A restraining order? Do you think that's going to stop me?" He spun, and faced off with Summer. "So you'll know, this was that one step over the line, Wendy. Now you won't even get monthly visitation. When I'm done with you, you're going to prison."

Now it was Rafe's turn to step forward. "You know, one of the good things about being an orthopedist is my ability to read bones, and bones never lie, *your honor*. Bone evidence holds up in court because it's brutally honest, it doesn't

conceal the secrets that lie beneath the surface…
like physical abuse. And the thing about bones is
that, while they heal, they leave behind scars of
their trauma…like broken wrists, broken cheek-
bones, cracked ribs. A good orthopedist can read
the difference between accidents and abuse."

For the first time Cameron actually blanched.

"And who knows what other bone truths we
might find in a complete body scan?" Rick
said. "As it turns out, my brothers and I own
the equipment that can do that scan. And I will
use it against you, if you ever…*ever* come near
Summer again."

"That whole brother thing," Jess said, his face
dead serious. "We stick together. Take care of
our own, and Summer and Alyssa are part of
our own. And if you don't believe we're prepared to back our words with action…" He deferred back to Rick.

"I have a couple of friends I'd like you to meet."
Rick stepped back and allowed Henry Danforth
to round the corner. But Henry wasn't alone.
With him was Amy's father, Joe Cavanaugh,
family court judge, New York. "This is my attorney, Henry Danforth, who, for the record, is

Summer's attorney," Rick said, "just so you'll know who all are coming at you. And something else you should know is that Henry's going to be asking you, in a nice way, to relinquish custody of your daughter on the grounds that you're an abuser. We're hoping that's what you decide to do. But if you don't, he'll fight you the ugly way."

"We all will," Rafe said. "Because we know what it takes to derail an abuser and Jess and I will take particular pleasure in derailing you."

"On that note," Rick continued, "let me introduce the parent of one of Summer's patients. Judge Joe Cavanaugh. In case you're interested, he's the one who issued the restraining order."

"Because I care about Summer," Joe said. "She's taken good care of my daughter these last weeks, and anybody who hurts her indirectly hurts Amy. And I just can't allow that to happen."

"So this is what you get to go up against, Cameron," Rick continued. "And so you'll see it coming, *we don't lose.*" He stepped back in line with his brothers, Jess on his left, Rafe on his right, then Henry and Joe took their places in that line, one on either end.

They were doing this for her, and as Summer watched the confrontation unfold, she was so full of emotion over what Rick had done that she didn't know whether to laugh or cry. "They *don't* lose, Cameron," she said for a lack of anything else to say. "They're a strong family, and they stick together."

Cameron took several steps forward, not to confront the men but to get into Summer's face. "You're bargaining with your daughter, Wendy," he said, his voice so low she would barely hear it. "Is that what you want? To wage this battle against me and hurt...what is it you call her now? Alyssa? Anyway, I will tell *Alyssa* exactly what you are...every last detail of it."

"But she knows what you are, Cameron," she countered, for the first time in her life holding her ground. "She saw you hit me."

"She doesn't know what she saw."

"If that's what you believe, then you're a stupid, *stupid* man."

Those were the words that flipped on the switch in Cameron, turning him from a man who was barely in control to one who didn't care who was there, watching him. In the blink of an eye his hand came up to strike her. But also in that same blink of an eye all three Corbett brothers jumped forward to stop him. Rick got there first, grabbed Cameron's arms so hard the man yelped. Then withdrew his hand and cradled it to his chest as Rafe and Jess took their places on either side of him, nearly pinning him in on himself.

"I'll sue you."

"For what?" Joe Cavanaugh asked. "Defending Summer? Because I saw the whole thing, and I'm willing to put aside my judge robes to testify." He held up his cellphone. "Or show somebody a video I've been shooting."

"That's not legal."

Joe turned to Jess. "Did I have your permission to videotape your cabin?"

Before Jess had the chance to answer, Rick lunged at Cameron with such a force it slammed him back into the wall. Then he held him there. "If you ever...*ever* touch her again..." He sucked in a sharp breath, fighting to regain in his temper. "This is where it ends, Cameron. Today, now, this is the end of it." He took two steps back. "If you want a long, public battle, I'm in. Lots of attention. Lots of noise. Lots of speculation and public exposure about who you are and what you really do. And when we make the claim of spousal abuse stick…which will make people wonder if you're fit to remain a judge for starters, or could even result in the suspension of your license to practice law, well, all I can say is, *choose what you love most, Cameron.*" He turned, actually gave Summer a wink, then refocused on Cameron. "It's a one-time deal on the table, and the minutes are ticking off your clock." He took another few steps backwards, this time not averting his stare. "You heard me. Choose what you love."

At that moment Henry Danforth broke the tenseness in the room by pulling a document from his pocket then stepping forward. "If it turns out you love your public image more than your ex-wife and daughter, sign on the dotted line. One signature, and we're on our way to being through with this mess."

"Sign it without reading it?' Cameron snapped,

still standing with his back to the wall. "Do you think I'm an idiot to sign it without reading it?"

"It's the promise to relinquish your rights to Alyssa, the real legalities to follow. That's all," Joe Cavanaugh stated. "Not binding, but a starter protection for Henry's client. Drew it up myself, actually. Least I could do to help Summer, because I want to keep her here, just like everybody else does. And I have a *personal* interest in that."

"Joe," Summer said, smiling. "I'm so grateful."

"Amy's doing better every day, so I'm the one who's grateful, Summer. Why else would I be here, ready to slam Judge Carson to the wall again, if that's what it takes?"

"You people are all crazy!" Cameron grumbled, grabbing the paper from Henry's hand. "The bunch of you...you deserve each other!"

"Actually, I think we do," Summer replied. "In ways you'd never understand."

"And you can all go to hell," Cameron said, seething. His voice so quiet it was barely audible. A vein was popping out on his neck, in striking contrast to his red face. And his hands were shaking as he scanned the document, then scrawled a very angry signature at the bottom and shoved it back at Henry. Without another word Judge Cameron Carson stormed past Rick, bumping hard into his shoulder. Then through the wall created by Rafe and Jess…a wall that bumped him back even harder in their brother's defense. And on out the door.

"Well, it looks like we know who Cameron loves more," Henry pronounced, then turned to Summer. "With this document, he's consented to give up *all* parental claims to Alyssa and to quit stalking you, on the condition that you won't prosecute him for the abuses you've suffered. Usually, I'm all for going after people like him, but in this case I believe we need to do this like Joe outlined to protect Alyssa from the publicity that might come of it. If any of this goes public, it could hurt her."

"Which means you win, Summer," Rick said, taking his place at her side and slipping his arm around her waist. "You win…*everything*."

"Everything," she said, and suddenly it was like the weight of an entire granite mountain lifted from her shoulders. She didn't need the legal papers to prove it. Seeing Cameron defeated, hearing the slam of the door behind him, feeling Rick's steady arm around her, knowing that the people here had come together as a family to protect her...that *was* everything. She looked up at the man she loved with her whole heart. After running and hiding for more than two years, Summer Adair was finally free.

EPILOGUE

"HE's anxious to have a little sister?"

Rick laughed. "I think Chris has big plans for that. Apparently, there are a lot of things a big brother's supposed to teach his little sister, and we've got lists."

"Lists. Well, Alyssa hasn't made any lists, but she does have some expectations, and her new father is included in quite a few of them."

"New father." He beamed with pride. "I like the sound of it. Can't wait until it happens." Joe Cavanaugh was expediting the adoption process, and they were expecting word shortly after their "*I do*".

"Neither can I," Summer said. "I've been a little worried the kids might not adjust, but so far they're good. Oh, and just so you'll know, Chris is taking over the house remodeling end of this family. He's decided he's going to supervise the project to make sure we get all the rooms we need. Or so he told me."

"My son…the master manipulator. What he means is that he's going to keep a close eye on the construction of the game room. That's where he has big plans."

"I'm glad we're going to add on to my house instead of moving somewhere off the estate. It's nice, knowing we'll have so much family within shouting distance, and lots of little cousins for Chris and Alyssa to play with." She smiled. "And another one on the way." Referring to Jess and Julie's soon-to-be addition to the Corbett clan.

"Maybe another one or two for us, too?" he asked.

"Definitely another one or two for us." Her baby, or babies, with Rick. More of her dream coming true.

"So, now the next important thing, since we've established that the kids will be OK."

"And that would be?" Summer asked.

"Your name. I think you should keep it," Rick said. It was a beautiful day. The sky was a perfect azure blue with white clouds in contrast. "Wendy is who you were to *him*." The name they would never speak again. "But Summer is who you are to me. And I love you as Summer."

"Grace gave me that name, actually. I used a couple of other ones before I met her, but this name…" She smiled. "It was a family name, not on the Corbett side, though. Summer Adair was *her* favorite cousin and best friend growing up, and I've loved it, felt special that she gave it to me, so I am Summer. And I'm living Summer's life."

"Aunt Grace gave you that name because she knew you were going to be part of the family, and that you'd honor the name."

Sighing, Summer laid her head over on Rick's shoulder. "Alyssa was my mother's middle name. When we ran away, Marielle…my daughter's birth name, by the way…was only two. I needed some kind of connection to something good in my life, or to someone I loved, so I gave her my mother's middle name because I figured *he* wouldn't know it, and every time I changed my name, I couldn't change hers because it was the one thing, the only thing that gave me any hope."

"It's a beautiful name."

"I want to add the middle name Grace. Alyssa Grace…" She paused. "Navarro or Corbett?"

"I'm Rick Navarro. By blood I'm a Corbett, but I'll keep my mother's name. You helped me with that, Summer. Made me understand the things I couldn't, made me realize that the world isn't a black or white place, that we all make choices, some good, some because that's what we believe we have to do. I am Maria Navarro's son, and I honor that. I only wish she could have known…"

"She knows, Rick," Summer said, stroking his cheek. "She knew who you were and in that she knew you would find your way. Understanding what she did was part of that journey, and she raised you strong so you could face that journey when you were ready. So she does know. And for your mother, Alyssa Grace Navarro it is. Has a nice sound to it, doesn't it?"

"Summer Adair Navarro sounds pretty good, too." He pulled her into his chest and lowered his lips to hers. "I'm glad we can do this now. It's been hell, restraining myself."

"Hell for me, too," she said, as the hard press of his lips silenced the rest of his words, and her lips parted beneath Rick's in the most natural of ways, like they'd been intimate lovers for ever and this moment was but one in some far larger destiny they shared. One brief kiss was what she promised herself at the start of it since this was, after all, their wedding day, and there was so much more to come later on. But even before the kiss began she was so hot for him she lost all control to pull back, or think, or even breathe normally. That's what he did to her. What she wanted from him. And it came with so much promise of everything else they would have. So she gave herself over to the full sensation when he ran his hands up her back, pulling her even closer to him into a tantric position of face to face, chest to chest, pelvis to pelvis, where she kissed him hard, with all the pent-up emotions forcing their escape.

Rick's tongue eagerly welcomed hers in the same sensation of heat and fury, and probed deeply, setting her entire body on fire. She wanted him here and now, like she'd never wanted another man, but she would wait, because in just an hour family and friends would gather at Gracie stables to celebrate Dr and Mrs Rick Navarro into their new life as husband and wife and family of four. "Rick," she murmured, as his kisses trailed down her throat. "Now that you've got me out here on your boulder, how are you going to get me off of it, because I have a wedding to attend in a little while?"

He smiled. "Maybe I won't."

"I think I like the sound of that. But Rafe and Jess are both expecting to stand up with their brother, along with Chris, and I don't want to disappoint them. And I have a couple of new sisters and a daughter who expect to stand alongside me. And Molly, my new niece. She's been making wedding plans as flower girl for days. There's no way I want to disappoint her, even though I do like the prospect of being out here on your boulder just a little while longer." She smiled. "It's hard to believe that I went from having only Alyssa to having…well, all the Corbetts, past, present and future."

"I know the feeling," he said, pointing to the spot where he'd inscribed his name years ago.

"When did you do that?"

He smiled. "A few days ago. It didn't seem right any more the way it was, so I came out here to fix it."

What was once a bare signature now read *Rick Navarro and Summer Adair...for ever.* "For ever," she murmured against his lips. She was home for ever. "So, let's go get married!"

"Or maybe," he said, "let the wedding come to us." He pointed to the whole lot of Corbetts and friends, all trudging their way up the trail, carrying flowers and picnic baskets and bottles of champagne.

"Right here?" she asked. "Really?"

"Right here. Our spot. Our family."

"Our family," she murmured, indulging in one more kiss before she climbed down off the boulder with Rick to begin their life together. "Our... everything." *Rick Navarro and Summer Adair... for ever.*

* * * * *

Mills & Boon® Large Print
Medical

September

FALLING FOR THE SHEIKH SHE SHOULDN'T	Fiona McArthur
DR CINDERELLA'S MIDNIGHT FLING	Kate Hardy
BROUGHT TOGETHER BY BABY	Margaret McDonagh
ONE MONTH TO BECOME A MUM	Louisa George
SYDNEY HARBOUR HOSPITAL: LUCA'S BAD GIRL	Amy Andrews
THE FIREBRAND WHO UNLOCKED HIS HEART	Anne Fraser

October

GEORGIE'S BIG GREEK WEDDING?	Emily Forbes
THE NURSE'S NOT-SO-SECRET SCANDAL	Wendy S. Marcus
DR RIGHT ALL ALONG	Joanna Neil
SUMMER WITH A FRENCH SURGEON	Margaret Barker
SYDNEY HARBOUR HOSPITAL: TOM'S REDEMPTION	Fiona Lowe
DOCTOR ON HER DOORSTEP	Annie Claydon

November

SYDNEY HARBOUR HOSPITAL: LEXI'S SECRET	Melanie Milburne
WEST WING TO MATERNITY WING!	Scarlet Wilson
DIAMOND RING FOR THE ICE QUEEN	Lucy Clark
NO.1 DAD IN TEXAS	Dianne Drake
THE DANGERS OF DATING YOUR BOSS	Sue MacKay
THE DOCTOR, HIS DAUGHTER AND ME	Leonie Knight

December

SYDNEY HARBOUR HOSPITAL: BELLA'S WISHLIST — Emily Forbes
DOCTOR'S MILE-HIGH FLING — Tina Beckett
HERS FOR ONE NIGHT ONLY? — Carol Marinelli
UNLOCKING THE SURGEON'S HEART — Jessica Matthews
MARRIAGE MIRACLE IN SWALLOWBROOK — Abigail Gordon
CELEBRITY IN BRAXTON FALLS — Judy Campbell

January

SYDNEY HARBOUR HOSPITAL: MARCO'S TEMPTATION — Fiona McArthur
WAKING UP WITH HIS RUNAWAY BRIDE — Louisa George
THE LEGENDARY PLAYBOY SURGEON — Alison Roberts
FALLING FOR HER IMPOSSIBLE BOSS — Alison Roberts
LETTING GO WITH DR RODRIGUEZ — Fiona Lowe
DR TALL, DARK...AND DANGEROUS? — Lynne Marshall

February

SYDNEY HARBOUR HOSPITAL: AVA'S RE-AWAKENING — Carol Marinelli
HOW TO MEND A BROKEN HEART — Amy Andrews
FALLING FOR DR FEARLESS — Lucy Clark
THE NURSE HE SHOULDN'T NOTICE — Susan Carlisle
EVERY BOY'S DREAM DAD — Sue MacKay
RETURN OF THE REBEL SURGEON — Connie Cox